Surviving Ryan

*Ryan was a gift from God to all of us
and now he is a gift to God*

Pamela Ferguson

xulon PRESS

Surviving Ryan
by Pamela Ferguson

Printed in the United States of America

Library of Congress Control Number: 2002117032
ISBN 9781591603696

Unless otherwise indicated, Bible quotations are taken from The Holy Bible: New International Version. Copyright © 1973 by the International Bible Society.

www.xulonpress.com

Candi and Taylor,

Thanks for all
your loving support.

P

Table of Contents

Thank you Ryan

Ryan, a friend and son of many
A brother, a confidante and supporter
Always a laugh, a joke, a smile and a
wave of your hand
You touched people old and young
with your effervescence.

From jokes as a little boy in the dug-out, on the
basketball court, on the playground
or delivering a pizza
Leave it to you Ryan to brighten our days.

Friends and family in their grief...
No, no, not Ryan. It couldn't be
A life so young and full
A future so bright
A shining star now so far away
You have shone on us all
An example in your absence
of how precious life is,
And how you made a difference.

Thank you for sharing your glow
You will continue to shine brightly.
Be that star in the sky
for your mom, dad, Graham, Brady and Dane.
They will be forever looking for you.

We will miss you so,
John, Hillary, Steve and Nick Thomas

Introduction

We are living every parent's nightmare. The phone rang. Our child was unconscious. We rushed to the hospital and the doctors told us he probably wouldn't make it. Then he died.

A year later, it still feels unbelievable, but we have made it a year. This book is about Ryan and the story of how he lived his life joyfully. It is also the story of how we lost him and how we learned to survive the loss. It is the story of the friends and family who helped us through what no parent ever wants to face, what really helped and what didn't help at all. It is meant to be a heartfelt guide to the grieving and to those who love them.

On June 3rd, 2000, our second son, Graham, played shortstop for Villa Park High School in Dodger Stadium for the state championship baseball finals and they won! Ryan had been home from the University of Arizona for three weeks. He was at the game along with our two youngest boys, Brady and Dane, grandparents, aunts, uncles, cousins and friends. For our family, since we had yet to have a wedding or a college graduation, it was our most exciting high. What we didn't know was that three weeks later, on June 25th, we would experience the most devastating low imaginable.

I am a marriage and family therapist. I'd been in private practice eighteen years when Ryan died. I had helped countless families through the loss of a loved one. I understand it so differently now. Our family has always been so very close but, losing Ryan has taught us all to cherish relationships even more, to be even closer. As Brady said, "the pain we feel at losing him is unspeakable." I am a more compassionate person and therapist; a better friend and parent, and a more loving wife now and I'd trade it all in a heartbeat to have him back. But that is not an option. I have a newly defined perspective of what is really important in life. I choose to survive in a meaningful way and by doing so; I believe I honor Ryan by trying to live my life as he did, joyfully. I have found strength in myself that I never knew I possessed. At a time when I have never felt more broken, I have also never felt more blessed.

Obituary

Ferguson, Ryan Bruce (age 21) died suddenly after suffering a cerebral hemorrhage caused by a heatstroke. A student at the University of Arizona in Tucson, majoring in Communications, he planned to graduate next year. People were drawn to Ryan by his ready smile, they stayed to enjoy his sense of humor and share his zest for life, earning him richness in friends beyond his years. More than anything, Ryan loved being the big brother and friend. His passions were Snowboarding, being at "The River," counseling at Y.M.C.A. camp and playing baseball. Ryan is loved dearly, and is survived by his parents: Bruce and Pam Ferguson; his three younger brothers: Graham, Brady and Dane; grandparents, aunts, uncles, cousins and friends.

A memorial service will be held at Trinity United Presbyterian Church in Tustin/Santa Ana on Thursday, June 29th at 3:00.

In lieu of flowers, please send contributions to: The Ryan Ferguson Foundation P.O. Box 3212, Orange, CA 928570212.

The monies will be used to establish a scholarship for Y.M.C.A. Camp Bluff Lake campers and for the Villa Park High School Baseball Program.

Before

My journal entry, July 7, 2000

*I*t has been twelve days since Ryan died. Twelve days and no minutes. I wasn't counting the days and minutes until Dane told me he was. I still can't believe Ryan is gone. How can a healthy twenty-one-year old have a heatstroke?

I knew though. I knew it was an emergency for me when my pager went off in Santa Barbara with the Grants' phone number. I knew when I saw the blood bubbling in his nose and mouth. I knew when they gave us a private room with a social worker and asked if we wanted a chaplain. I knew he was going to die. I knew when the neurosurgeon said, "He's not brain dead yet" that our Ryan was already gone. I knew even as I asked him to wake up that it was too late.

There are six of us...four boys, Bruce and me. They are a unit, two and two. We're even on the chair lifts. How could we have gotten Ryan safely to twenty-one and then lose him. I can't ask "why"....that will never help. I just have to accept that he's gone to heaven. God needs young angels too.

June 24, 2000 7:15 P.M.

I was in Santa Barbara for the weekend celebrating my mom's seventy-fifth birthday with my sister, Candi. My pager went off as soon as we were seated for dinner. It was my brother-in-law, Taylor. "Ryan has been in a motorcycle accident. The brain scan looks okay but he is still unconscious and they've taken him to Loma Linda Hospital."

We left the restaurant immediately and I thought of the vague uneasiness I'd felt all afternoon. My pager went off again. This time it was Matt and Josh, the friends who were dirt-bike riding with Ryan. "There was no accident. He didn't hit his head. He said he felt hot so we were on our way back to the truck when he fell over, unconscious. He's just hot. As soon as they get him hydrated, he'll be okay. They took him to Loma Linda from San Gorgonio because they have specialists in heatstroke. He'll be okay."

I was trying to understand everything that had happened and to gather information that I could pass on to the doctors. This was the time to face any possibility that might be important and so I asked, "Were you guys drinking or doing drugs?"

"We were drinking water and Gatorade. Ryan was leading the way back when he fell off the dirt bike unconscious. They think he broke his arm but he didn't hit his head." Josh had gone back to get the truck and Matt had stayed with Ryan when he collapsed holding his tongue with his finger. They had dragged him into the shade, took off his clothes and tried to pour water on him. Their cell phones didn't work until they reached the highway and by then they were right by San Gorgonio Hospital so they drove him straight there. They went through his wallet and found his insurance card and emergency numbers to call. This was how they got my pager number.

I reassured the boys that they had done everything right and thanked them. It sounded better than the first story of a motorcycle accident but I now understood that Ryan had been unconscious more than four hours. We packed so quickly leaving the hotel that we didn't get all our stuff. I started to try to make phone calls, had no cell phone service and ended up throwing up in the bushes. I couldn't reach Bruce as my sister drove from Santa Barbara to Loma Linda. Graham, 18, and Brady, 16, both worked with some of Ryan's friends at local pizza parlors. They were now at home and I reassured them that there had not been an accident, no head injury. Dane, 14, was at Angel stadium with his baseball coach. Bruce was on a one-day horseback ride in Temecula and was out of cell phone range. I couldn't remember the name of the friends where Bruce was having dinner even though I'd known them for years. When I finally remembered, no one answered the phone. I reached Dane's coach's wife and asked her to get Dane home so the boys would be together. I had this sense of urgency that the boys needed to all be together and then they could keep trying to reach Bruce.

By now, my nephew, Carter, had arrived at the hospital. He was eight months younger than Ryan and they were more like twins than cousins. Ryan was still unconscious and they wouldn't let Carter stay with him. He would be our liaison at the hospital. The hospital had given Carter a room to wait in. I didn't like the seriousness that implied.

It was 11:00 by the time we reached the freeway exit to the hospital and Bruce finally was in cell phone range. He was about fifteen minutes from home pulling a horse trailer. He'd drop off the horse, get the boys and come.

Carter led me into the emergency room to see Ryan, an image I will never forget. Here was my beautiful handsome son, twenty-one years old, lying so very still, on a respirator, with blood trickling from his nose and mouth. I kissed him and whispered to him as my heart sank, trying to boss him into consciousness, "It's Mom. I'm here. Wake up."

June 25th was the day we'd always celebrated Ryan's Christmas birthday and it was now almost midnight, "Happy Birthday!" I turned to the doctor and tried to calmly gather information even though I knew what he was going to say. "Is he critical?"

"Gravely critical."

I had never heard of a condition worse than critical but I knew this doctor was trying to begin to tell me that Ryan would die. I listened to what no parent ever wants to hear. "We think he's had a heatstroke. His temperature was 105 degrees when he got to San Gorgonio Hospital so that means it had been at least 106. He's in renal failure which made it difficult for him to breathe so San Gorgonio Hospital put him on a respirator. He's bleeding internally. The CAT scan they did looked fine but we want to do another one."

The doctors didn't understand why Ryan was suffering a cerebral hemorrhage since there was no apparent head injury. I told them that Ryan had had a virus two weeks earlier and had been put on antibiotics when he developed blisters on his tongue. The doctor then had told Ryan he was run-down and too thin. He needed to eat better, rest more and slow down. Ryan was the typical college student, working, taking classes and staying out late with friends. He'd been thin his whole life (6'3," 165 pounds) but had assured me this was the summer he'd "bulk" up. He'd been off medication for a week and was feeling fine. We'd been boosting his nutrition. The doctors and I discussed the possibility of meningitis but that didn't explain the cerebral hemorrhage.

Carter led the way to the chapel and Mom and I prayed for Ryan. When I came back to the emergency room, Ryan was going for the second CAT scan so I got to kiss him again. My sister and I waited in a different waiting room by the CAT scan elevator for some word. The E.R. doctor I quickly nicknamed "Dr. Grim" because of his bedside manner came out and told us, "Now we know what's wrong. Ryan's head is full of blood. He must have hit it when he fell. We're calling in a neurologist."

"Will he be okay?"

Very slowly and cautiously Dr. Grim said, "I have seen some patients survive something like this." His emphasis was clearly on "some."

Midnight. Bruce and the boys arrived and I took them back into the E.R. to see Ryan. I will never forget their horrified, tearful faces as they saw their big brother. Bruce was chalk white and still. Ryan was bleeding so much more now. The blood was streaming. I had been at the hospital for only an hour or so and it was obvious how much Ryan was deteriorating. Ten minutes later, the neurosurgeon came in and pulled Bruce and me out into the hall for a consultation. I didn't remember until much later that Carter was there, too. His name was Dr. Figueroa and I remember the softness of his voice, and the kindness in his eyes, as he showed us Ryan's CAT scan. "There is bleeding in his head and he has lost his ability to coagulate his blood. (I would later understand this is a condition called disseminating intravascular coagulation disease, commonly called D.I.C.) It's possible it's an aneurysm rather than a heatstroke. The bleeding is damaging his brain but we can't operate because he'll bleed to death and if we don't stop the bleeding, he'll be brain dead soon. The next hour is critical."

My knees buckled for the first time in my life. Bruce caught me as I hit the floor. "But this is our child," I wailed.

Bruce held me as Dr. Figueroa gently said, "I know that and I am so sorry. We are going to do everything we can. We're going to give him plasma to try to stop the bleeding. If we can get it stopped in the next hour, then we'll be able to operate and then we'll assess how much the blood has damaged the brain."

So Bruce and I went to tell the boys what the doctor had said. By now we had a chaplain and a social worker with us in our room. We sat the boys in a circle and told them that their brother was probably going to die. We prayed together. We told them that we were going to donate Ryan's organs because we knew that was what he wanted. We have never had a more painful family meeting. And then we began to take care of our boys. We told them how much we loved Ryan and how we would get through this together. We began to tell funny Ryan stories. I had a compelling need not to make Ryan a martyr, not to create this legacy they could never live up to. I felt helpless to change Ryan's outcome, Ryan was in God's hands, so I turned all my attention to helping our boys and Ryan's friends. Somehow, there was a gentle push from Ryan to do this.

By now, Ryan's friends were gathering in the parking lot of the hospital. I was deeply touched to see them there. These were young adults; some had been friends with Ryan since pre-school. We told them what the doctor had said and we cried together. All through that horrible night, more and more of Ryan's friends gathered. Each time I went out there, they were holding one of my boys, or kneeling in prayer. Their circle of friendship was an overwhelmingly tender show of love. One buddy held me in his arms and told me how much Ryan always knew he was loved and oh! How I needed to hear that!

As that long, sad night wore on, more grandparents, aunts and uncles arrived. I called our dear friends, Tim and Shelley, and told them the doctors thought Ryan would be brain dead soon.

"We're on our way."

Bruce and I kept checking on Ryan but they wouldn't let us be with him for long. He was moved up to the Trauma Unit. Ryan's elbow had been broken when he fell and I can remember thinking that he'd never pitch again. This was so foolish because Ryan hadn't pitched since his freshman year of college. I know that a part of me wanted that to be the problem, rather than the blood that was now streaming from his nose and mouth. At one point, Dr. Grim came in while I was whispering to Ryan and singing softly the songs of his childhood. "His head is full of blood. He can't hear you."

Dr. Grim froze at the look I gave him and shrank back, leaving the room quickly as I replied. "I have always been told that the hearing is the last to go. I'm going to talk to my son, sing to him and pray as long as he is still alive."

Our youngest son, Dane, put his arms around me when I went back into the hall and tried to be reassuring. "This is a very good hospital, Mom. Ryan's going to be okay."

"This is a good hospital, Daner, but I don't think Ryan will be okay." Oh, how his tender gesture at fourteen touched me.

Bruce and I snuck around a hospital corner at one point and sobbed in each other's arms. "How can we lose this child?" We thought we were out of the sight and earshot of our boys, but, when we rejoined our family, it was obvious by the stricken look on their faces that they had all heard.

A nurse stopped me as I came back into the hospital from the parking lot, "He's doing much better."

"My son?!"

"No, your father!" My dad's blood pressure had skyrocketed and he was now admitted to the hospital emergency room. Bruce and I went inside to find my dad, sheepishly hooked up to all kinds of monitors. We teased my dad about how helpful this was! There was a sweet, young nurse attending to my dad and she said, "I know about your son, can we pray together?" We bowed our heads as she prayed for our dying child.

And they brought their dogs! In the midst of our tragedy, we did see the humorous moments. My dad and stepmom, and Bruce's mom and her boyfriend, brought their dogs to the hospital when their grandson was dying! Bruce's mom forgot dog food so there was a lot of commotion dealing with the dogs. Could they borrow dog food?

The hospital gave us blankets and the boys slept for a few hours. Ryan was still alive in the morning and more people had arrived. For a time, it seemed that there might be hope because the plasma was improving his ability to coagulate blood.

I had been asking about his contacts during the night and his nurses told me he must not have been wearing them. That didn't seem right to me because Ryan usually wore them. The morning trauma nurses let us see Ryan for a minute. They found his contacts! I knew that focusing on his contacts was a lot like worrying that he'd never pitch again. I knew that even as I had asked. One nurse said that she'd be very scared if it were her son and I understood she was trying to prepare us.

The boys hadn't yet seen Ryan that morning but the doctors were in his room so we had to wait. The only time the five of us were alone at the hospital was that one time. Later, that would seem so very significant to me. We were in a tiny little waiting room next to the trauma unit and Bruce and I were telling our boys that if Ryan lived, he'd probably always need special care. We would all need to help. Our family discussion was interrupted by three doctors who came in to join us in this tiny little room. Dr. Grim was one of them but he didn't speak. The head trauma doctor stepped over the boys and knelt down to summarize everything that had happened to Ryan and told us that Ryan would die. I remember asking, "Who dies from a heatstroke?" and he answered that lots of people do. They were going to bring in a portable CAT scan to do one more test, but it was time for us to go say good-bye to our child.

A part of me felt like I was watching what was happening on many levels. I understood that the doctors meant that we'd be soon faced with a decision to turn off the respirator even though they didn't say that. The five of us circled around Ryan and we asked for a chaplain. My sister came in and we told her that Ryan was dying then so she went to get the other members of our family. I wanted to trade places with him so very much. I'd lived more than twice his number of years, "God, take me!" I also knew I didn't want to face living without him. They brought me a chair. We all prayed and told Ryan how much we loved him. Dane wanted to leave but I was afraid for him to be alone, afraid that if he missed this, it would be harder. I could see my nephew Travis' young bride, Sharie, watching me. I saw, in the reflection of her face, what a mother looks like who's losing a child.

The chaplain was delayed. The technicians came in with the CAT scan but the nurses waved them away. They wouldn't need it. I understood that that meant Ryan was dying right then. I was aware of my divorced parents taking politically correct turns hugging me. The chaplain still didn't come and it seemed like Ryan's dying went on forever. He jerked his arm and my dad showed me, thinking perhaps that Ryan was moving. I knew, though, that it was the end. There was a sudden release of blood and the nurse checked his eyes. One was fixed and dilated, the sign that he was brain dead. I never noticed the machines but Bruce saw that his pressure was dropping and bottoming out. We were ushered out and the chaplain finally arrived to this scene.

"What's going on?"

"Our son has just died, pray for us."

"There is always hope," the chaplain was trying to be encouraging. We told him again that Ryan was gone and he prayed together with us. Both Dane and my mom noted the time as 11:15 A.M. when Ryan had died but the doctors didn't pronounce him until 11:22. I could hear them working on him as we prayed but then they came out and said that

Ryan had died. We said again that we wanted to donate his organs but the head trauma doctor now told us that his high temperature had damaged the organs too much. Oh, how we wanted someone to have this young heart! It would make something good come from this tragedy but we couldn't donate anything.

Graham would later retell this story to one of my friends. "Each time we saw this doctor, the news was worse. Ryan is going to die. Ryan died. You can't donate his organs."

I ran to the bathroom to stifle my screams and washed my face again and again with cold water. I didn't recognize myself. My sister came to get me. Bruce and I could see Ryan, only us. We clung to each other as we walked into the hospital room to see our dead child. The doctor explained that because they had to do an autopsy, the respirator tubes and everything would still be connected. We both had enough medical knowledge to understand the extent of this autopsy. He was such an awful color, that color of death. We kissed him so gently even though our Ryan was no longer there. The same nurse who had told me that she'd be scared if it were her son helped us clip a lock of his hair. Bruce wrapped it carefully in a tissue and tucked it in his pocket.

They said we could bring the boys back in to see him. I found them huddled in the hospital hall crying with family and friends. I didn't think they needed to see him. They'd watched him die, wasn't that enough? He looked so very awful. The chaplain gently approached us and said it might help them later. They were old enough.

So our new family of five went in to see Ryan. We told the boys what he looked like first and stayed with him only briefly. Carter and Travis came in also. I'll always remember Carter's face right then. A young nurse stopped us on our way out and asked if we'd consider donating Ryan's tissue to burn victims. I'm not sure I'd ever heard of tissue donation before that moment. We agreed.

All I wanted to do was to go home. Natalie, the love of Ryan's life, was trying to get here from Dallas but hadn't arrived. Her mom reached me on the phone at the hospital and I told her that Ryan was already gone. I hurt so much for Natalie right then also. Her mom and I agreed that Natalie shouldn't see Ryan right now. She'd come to our house later to be with us. Months later, I would hear that Natalie reached Ryan's buddy, Marc, who was trying to get here from Utah. His plane had just landed when Natalie phoned.

"We didn't make it."

"You mean you missed your flight?"

"No, we didn't make it in time. Ryan died." Marc's mom found him curled up in a ball by baggage.

We called a few friends on the way home. Dane rode with us but never said a word. Some friends had just heard and were on their way to the hospital and just missed us. One girlfriend told me she saved my message for weeks. In our small community of Villa Park, word had quickly spread that Ryan was dying. One friend later told us that she was driving next to us over the hill to our home and could tell from the expression on my face that Ryan had died.

I had heard my dad telling the boys as we left the hospital, "Be strong for your mother."

"No, boys, we're going to take turns being strong for each other."

My journal entry, July 10th

I was reminded today of the noise I kept making when Ryan was dying and for the first few days afterwards. It was a deep, guttural wolf sound combined with the pant-blow breathing of childbirth. This sobbing cry was unrecognizable, even to me, and I was the one making the sound. This must be the sound of a mother's heart breaking.

After

Bruce, speaking at Ryan's service, on June 29th

*W*e *came home after spending the night at the hospital and we thought we'd just hunker down, just the five of us. But pretty soon our friends, Ryan's friends, Graham's friends, Brady's friends and Dane's friends were at our house. There must have been one hundred and fifty people at our house that first day and it's gone on like that for four days. We have been completely overwhelmed by the love and support you people have showered upon our family. Thank you.*

April, the daughter we never had, drove Graham and Brady home from the hospital. She seemed to instinctively understand what I needed. She stood outside my bathroom door while I showered. Bruce came to get me as I was drying off. The tissue bank was on the phone and needed information. I knelt on the floor in my bedroom, wrapped with one towel around me and another on my hair and gave them permission to take Ryan's tissue, corneas, heart valves, anything they could use. Then they recorded my answers as they questioned me about Ryan's health history, tattoos, sex life, and all this incredibly personal stuff that a mom isn't supposed to ever have to discuss. They again asked my permission. Our son had been dead such a short time and this was so difficult! While I was drying my hair, the coroner's office talked to Bruce and said they needed the heart valves and the corneas for the autopsy. It was as if the tissue bank and the coroner's office wanted us to mediate their argument and our son had just died! I remember thinking that some people would feel so overwhelmed by this that they'd withdraw permission. I managed to get my hair dry and get dressed, but contact lenses, make-up and shoes were beyond my capabilities that first day.

As April and I went downstairs, friends were already there, organizing food and soft drinks. My girlfriend, Janet, came over and I can remember her saying, "Now you're going to understand how many people in the community really love you." I don't know how she knew that, at that point, but it was one of the blessings of Ryan's passing that I would come to cherish.

People came. They came with more food. They came to offer comfort, hugs and prayer. They brought us letters. Each visit, each gesture, was a gift. Those were the gifts that got us through the first few days. Some gifts will be cherished forever. If we had only received one letter, we would have wanted it to be this one. It came that first day.

To the Ferguson Family:

I send sympathy and compassion. I thought I would share with you what Ryan did for my life. I have been sober for almost two years—-July 1, 1998 is my sobriety date. Ryan and I were dating at the time when I started heavily drinking and using drugs. He was very concerned about me and told me if I didn't stop, he couldn't be together with me. I continued to use drugs but hid it from him. It worked for a while but my addiction became obvious by the way I acted.

I dumped my friends, my grades went down the tubes, my family life became a wreck because of my actions, I quit the song-leading squad because I would rather be partying, etc. The reason I am sharing this with you is because Ryan is the one who told my parents that I had a problem. He broke up with me because I was choosing drugs over the relationship. A few weeks later, I went to a treatment center and I've been sober ever since. I got sober to save the relationship but ended up staying sober for myself. I got straight A's this semester in college, went to school in Hawaii and got certified as a personal trainer and aerobics instructor, and, most of all- I got my family back. The most beautiful thing is that I got to make amends to him before he passed. Without Ryan being a part of my life, I don't know where I would be today. Ryan saved my life and for that I am truly grateful.

Love, Allison

Alison called for Ryan just after we got home from the hospital and Bruce answered the phone. From then on, our friends answered the phones for us. We will never forget Allison's gift to us, because she was the first to open our eyes, to our son, the dedicated friend. We had only known a small part of this story from Ryan. We never knew he had gone to Allison's parents and Allison's willingness to share so very openly made us so very proud of Ryan, and of her!

On that first day, Graham pulled me aside, "Mom, you always said you could never survive it if something happened to one of us."

"Graham, I said that to provide each of you with an extra coat of protection. I wanted you to be so very careful. I never wanted to have to face something happening to one of you guys. But I will survive this; we will all survive this together." I knew then that Bruce and I had to show our boys how to go forward, how to survive this, how not to be broken by this, the question was how do we do that?

Read by Bruce at Ryan's service Excerpt from Jim Joffe's letter

Sunday was a reminder that our children are "on loan," and not really ours. The constant stream of so many friends through your home this week was a testament to the fact that Ryan belonged to all of us, each in a different way. We bring them into the world, and with that first "no" out of their little mouths, the independence we know they must develop begins. Day by day, they begin pulling away. We want them to become responsible, successful, self-sufficient young men, but not really today. Never just yet.

We never want to lose our little boys. Whether at 21, or 81, there is something inside of us that doesn't ever want to let go of any of them. So we keep our memories. Given the choice, we would rather have 21 years with him than none. Maybe your work was more finished than you think, on "such a nice young man."

My sister, Candi, at Ryan's service:

I've known Bruce since he was in high school, so I knew him well at this very same age. It was just about at age twenty-one, that Bruce had the chance to be the photographer for a book written by a dear college professor, Dr. Leo Buscaglia. It was a simple pictorial called <u>Because I am Human</u> and it goes something like this. "Because I am human, I can play, laugh, love, feel, hug. I can be sarcastic." That one wasn't in the book but I thought it worked well for Ryan.

When my sister asked me at the hospital, "How do we do this without Ryan?" I had no idea but I have watched in overwhelming awe all week as a loving community of family

and friends have already started. We have started by cel-
ebrating the life of Ryan and the memories of what we loved
to do with Ryan. Right now, we can only do this one moment
at a time, but the day will come when we can do it one week
at a time. I know this. Spiritual Ryan will be our guide and
smiling companion.

That first day, that Sunday, when we should have been
celebrating Ryan's half-birthday, we instead began to plan
for his funeral. We wanted to try to have the service on
Thursday since Saturday was my birthday and it was the July
4th weekend holiday. We also wanted him to be buried at the
local neighborhood cemetery. It suddenly seemed so very
important to have him close, as if we'd not have to completely let go. I wanted to be able to visit Ryan's grave and
this cemetery was only two miles away. Somehow I understood, from the very beginning, that I needed to have Ryan
close. We'd have to wait until the next day to find out if that
was possible since we're Presbyterian and it was a Catholic
cemetery. I prayed that it would work out.

As people came, we told the story over and over again.
In doing so, we began to process the unbelievable. It helped
us so to have people listen. Their presence was comforting. I
remember asking my friend, "What am I now? Am I still the
mother of four boys?"

Bruce pulled me aside and said we should all sleep in our
room that night. But, by 10:00 or so, when all our friends
were gone, the boys were downstairs with a whole group
of their friends watching videos. It seemed to be what they
needed so Bruce and I fell into each other's arms and tried
to sleep the exhausted sleep of heartbroken parents in shock.

Months later, in November, I dragged Bruce to a grief
seminar at church. We were the only people there who'd
lost a child, most people were newly widowed or had lost
a spouse, and our loss was so very different that the sem-

inar wasn't especially appropriate. However, a gentleman helping the speaker talked to us afterwards. His son had been hit and killed by a car at fourteen. What struck both of us was how he could still vividly describe the horror of that first night and his son had been gone more than thirty years!

Dane awakened us in the middle of the night and we went in to check on Brady and Graham. Those two brothers were wrapped in each other's arms sleeping in one bed. I will never forget their tender vulnerability. I know I will still see this image thirty years from now.

The next day was Monday and Tim and Shelley came over early. They'd already been to Holy Sepulcher to find out if being Catholic was a requirement to being buried there. It wasn't! Tim said that he'd taken the week off and they'd be there to help in any way they could. I reached Dr. Bob Pietsch at church and made tentative arrangements for the service to be Thursday afternoon, pending the autopsy. Jeff Wagner, our neighbor next door for the first nine years of Ryan's life, was the youth minister. Jeff would do the service with Bob Pietsch. The boys didn't want to go with us to the mortuary or the cemetery.

As Tim, Shelley, Bruce and I left to make the sad arrangements; Bruce saw that Ryan's wallet and cell phone were on our front table, left there by Josh or Matt. He opened Ryan's wallet and let out such a wounded cry that I came running. He had found a much dog-eared copy of "Footprints." We didn't know Ryan carried that with him and it was such a gift that morning as we left for the mortuary. What a testimony to Ryan's faith and that God was with us now! I now see it as the first "sign" from Ryan.

One night a man had a dream. He dreamed he was walking along the beach with the LORD. Across the sky flashed scenes from his life. For each scene, he noticed two sets of footprints in the sand; one belonging to him and the other to the LORD.

31

When the last scene of his life flashed before him, he looked back at the footprints in the sand. He noticed that many times along the path of his life there was only one set of footprints. He also noticed that it happened at the very lowest and saddest times in his life.

This really bothers him and he questioned the LORD about it. "LORD, you said that once I decided to follow you, you'd walk with me all the way. But I have noticed that during the most troublesome times in my life, there is only one set of footprints. I don't understand why, when I needed you most, you would leave me."

The LORD replied, "My precious, precious child, I love you and I would never leave you. During your times of trial and suffering, when you see only one set of footprints, it was then I carried you."

When it came time to buy Ryan's coffin, we walked into a showroom. I made it a few feet and felt my legs go out from under me. Poor Bruce! As Shelley led me out, I was calling over my shoulder, just a plain lining, no roses, no patterns, not blue! I gave way to deep, wrenching sobs then. We were picking out our son's coffin! Bruce invited me back in gently to see his choice. It was beautiful. He later told me that he'd wanted the coffin to be oak because of its strength and value but there wasn't one that he'd liked. This one was poplar and, at first, he hesitated because poplar is not considered a fine wood and not as strong as oak. But then he remembered that poplar trees grow on the banks of rivers and grew to be tall and lean. Poplar trees bend and sway in the wind. Our tall, lean Ryan loved to be at the river and had adapted to every challenge life presented to him. So it seemed such an appropriate choice.

I was ready to order Ryan's headstone then. Larry, the mortician, gave us excellent advice. He encouraged us to wait until later. He told us that this would be our most visible decision and advised us to walk around the cemetery in the weeks to follow. We'd come up with an idea then. He also let us know that we should pay an honorarium to each of the ministers, the church itself and any musicians. We wouldn't have known that.

At that moment, the autopsy was not yet scheduled and no one could be reached at the coroner's office. Larry thought the service might need to be delayed until after the July 4th holiday. That would just drag it out so! This was still unsettled as we drove to the cemetery to make the arrangements. I was aware of the tremendous costs we were accumulating. This would take all the money we had set aside for Ryan's last year of college! My dad had asked me if we had a family plot. We were busy paying for Ryan's college and planning for the younger boys' education. It had never occurred to us that we'd be needing cemetery spaces. I worriedly whispered to Bruce, "We're just going to buy a plot for Ryan, right?"

Bruce, at that moment saw the bigger picture. "We're going to buy a plot for us right next to Ryan. We are going to be with Ryan."

The coroner's office finally reached Bruce when we were at the cemetery. My sweet husband took the phone outside and the next thing we knew, the autopsy was scheduled for Tuesday.

Our house was filling up with people when we got back. Flowers were being delivered again and again. These flowers were so very beautiful but they'd be gone soon. With the help of our friends and family, we developed the idea to establish a foundation in Ryan's memory that would support Villa Park High School Baseball and camperships to the Orange Y.M.C.A. Camp Bluff Lake. Ryan was a left-handed pitcher in high school. He had started going to Bluff Lake as a young camper and matured into a counselor, always taking the youngest campers. This seemed to be such a fitting way to honor his memory.

We scheduled a meeting at the church the next morning to plan Ryan's service. We'd accomplished so much that day. The obituary had to be written and delivered to the mortuary with the clothes Ryan would wear by 2:00 the next day. My girlfriend, Janet, also took the week off. She'd been president of every P.T.A. our kids had ever been in. She took on the arduous task of organizing the reception at our house after Ryan's Thursday service. We nicknamed her our "Funeral Franc" after "Franc" in the movie "Father of the Bride" who planned weddings. We couldn't have had a better "Funeral Franc" than Janet.

Food kept arriving and someone always made sure I ate. At one point, I realized that there were people sitting in my living room who hadn't spoken to each other in years. It is amazing how a tragedy unites people.

One man walked into the house and I didn't recognize him at all. It turned out that we had a plumbing problem and he was there to fix it. Real life doesn't exactly stop, even in tragedy!

Late that night, when all our visitors were gone, the five of us went to Ryan's room to find clothes for him to wear. Ryan hadn't lived at home in three years and so Graham had taken over the prime real estate of Ryan's old room at that time. Ryan had now been home, for the first time in three years, since mid May. He was in Graham's old room and his stuff had not exactly been put away and organized in the six weeks he'd been home. Since he had an internship at a commercial real estate company for the summer, his good Dockers pants were dry-cleaned and ready to roll. But we had to make sure he was buried in the right navy blue blazer. Anyone with lots of boys will especially appreciate this dilemma. Ryan had flown home from Tucson in February for my stepdad's seventy-fifth birthday celebration. As we were arriving at the party, Ryan pulled on his blazer and realized it was probably his much shorter roommate's jacket. Ryan conned Brady into switching jackets because Brady is just as lean but not as tall, besides, Ryan was the oldest brother and he made up all the rules. Anyhow, we didn't think Ryan had ever straightened out the "switched-blazer problem" because his roommate said he had his own jacket. We had all the boys try on all the navy blue blazers we owned to find the one that fit each of them best because it probably didn't make that much difference how Ryan's jacket fit.

Ron Clear, at Ryan's service, understood that a eulogy is also meant to comfort the grieving family:

A great person once said that if a man died and left behind five real friends, then he had a great life. Looking around at all of you it is clear that Ryan had a very great life. Although he had a short life, everyone who knew him, knows he lived every moment to the fullest. I had the honor of working with Ryan at YMCA camp. Seeing him grow from an awkward, squirrelly kid, into a wonderful young man who was confident, charismatic, kind and loving.

Most of all, Ryan had a very spiritual side to him. He believed that Camp was a set-point for him each year, allowing him to get refocused and reminding him of the man he wanted to grow up to be. The YMCA was a place where Ryan could be himself—not afraid to shed tears or to pull pranks. And it was a place where he would form friendships for a lifetime.

The two people, who were his best friends, were also his parents. He loved them completely. From his mom, he got his wisdom and sense of purpose. Ryan could always make you feel better when you were down, and always made you feel welcome. I never knew of anyone who walked away from Ryan not feeling a little bit better than before. From his dad, he got his zest for life and his motivation. Ryan loved life and wanted to be successful like his father; not just as a pro-

fessional, but as a complete man. *He respected and looked up to his dad.*

As for his brothers, no one could love them more. My last conversation with Ryan was all about how proud he was of each one of his brothers. He had just seen Graham playing baseball and his team win C.I.F. He was proud of Graham. He had seen Graham grow into a confident and responsible young man. He was very proud of his brother becoming a counselor this year at camp. Brady, the intellectual one... Ryan respected him for not following the others, but for being his own man. Ryan also wished he was as slick as Brady with the girls. Dane....the youngest of the Fergusons but not the smallest. (Dane and Ryan were the tallest brothers, both 6'3" tall, when Ryan died.) He has the body of a grown man but the heart of a warm child. He was so proud of Dane for his accomplishments and for the way Dane is. He knew that Dane was a person of many thoughts but few words.

Ryan was a gift from God to all of us, and now he is a gift to God. We will miss Ryan and we will never forget him.

My sister, Candi, came over early on Tuesday morning and we wrote the obituary. We included information about the foundation which meant that Candi had to set up a P.O. Box that morning as well so donations could be mailed to it. But we forgot to mention where and when the service would be which is the point of getting the obituary in the paper before the service. Thankfully, I realized this while I was showering and so we added this critical information before it was sent to the newspaper.

We also planned the memorial brochure. I had saved a brochure that a friend had done for his dad's service because it was so lovely. I knew just where it was but I always thought we'd use it for a parent, never our child. We copied that format and my sister, a computer whiz, put together this beautiful tribute to Ryan including "Footprints," a poem I wrote to Ryan "Secrets of Motherhood" when he'd graduated from high school, pictures, his nicknames, "Ryanisms" and a poem delivered to us by a dear friend.

Read by Bruce at Ryan's service: Excerpt from
Katie O'Connor's letter:

Ryan was one of those guys who was easily recognized as being special. Just watching him and the way that he treated other people made everyone want to get to know him. At camp, I watched all of his campers just gravitate towards him, and it always inspires me seeing the reaction that all of you brothers have when you are together. He made an impression on everyone that he came in contact with, and after knowing him, it was impossible not to aspire to be like him. So many people that I know, want to be the friend that Ryan was to other people, or offer the same energy that he did to being a camp counselor. He is one in a million and I am sure that he will never be forgotten. His fun-loving personality shows in all of you. I think the world of your family and I wanted you to know that you guys will always be in my prayers.

The five of us went together to plan Ryan's service with Bob Pietsch. He suggested that we limit the eulogies to not more than four speakers. We decided that Bruce's brother, Jim, Ron Clear (the director of the Y.M.C.A. camp), my sister, Candi, and Bruce would speak. He suggested that anyone who was eulogizing Ryan would do best if they wrote down their thoughts. Bruce wanted to honor Ryan by speaking but I wasn't sure, actually until he did, that he'd be able to talk.

We also talked about ways to control opening up the eulogies to anyone. We felt the service would be too long if we did that. It was decided that Jeff would announce that everyone would have an opportunity to share their memories by writing them down. April knew a soloist who had met Ryan and would sing. We had to figure out what songs we wanted. This was a concession for Bruce because we had sung together at his dad's funeral and he wanted us to sing at Ryan's service. I didn't think we'd be able to do that. A guitarist, who played "Dave Matthews' type" music, would provide background music before the service began.

I felt that it was really important that we have an open casket. The shock of losing Ryan so suddenly was unbelievable. Perhaps it would bring some closure to Ryan's friends to have an open casket. After much discussion and several phone calls, we decided to have the casket open after the service for anyone who wanted to view the body. It would be in the narthex or foyer of the church but not open in the sanctuary during the service. Although I was initially disappointed with this decision, I later decided it was a "God thing" and was so very grateful that the casket had been closed during the service. It gave people a choice and it made it easier for us to participate in the celebration of Ryan's life. These suggestions along with the mortician's information about the honorarium and waiting to order the headstone, were really the only advice we received on how to have a funeral and reception.

It was during this meeting, that I started shaking and I knew I needed to call my doctor for a prescription. I didn't want the boys to be haunted by images of their mom collapsing at Ryan's funeral. My doctor prescribed something for anxiety and for sleep, cautioning me about being responsible and not to combine it with alcohol. I carefully doled out these prescriptions over the next year when I needed help.

More friends and family were at our house when we returned from the church. Ryan's service was a total team effort. Some were in charge of making picture posters to be displayed at the church and then again at our house. These posters had blown-up pictures of Ryan at all different ages with wonderful captions. They were perfect.

Bruce and Tim left for the mortuary to deliver Ryan's clothes and to handle a few details. They later told me that while the autopsy was now completed, Ryan's body was still at the morgue and they were going to go get Ryan if they had to be the ones to deliver him to the mortuary. This never needed to happen but it gave the guys something they could control at that moment, when clearly everything was out of control.

We also finalized the list of pall bearers. We were unable to limit it to less than twelve and even that, was so very difficult to do. Ryan had so many good, good friends.

By Wednesday morning, it was decided that my nephew, Crosby, and Brady would make a video to be shown at the reception for Ryan. Since this is Bruce's business, Crosby went to the office to learn how to use this kind of video editing machine. Crosby and Brady stayed up all night with the help of a lot of friends to make this video. They used Dave Matthews' music and the eight-and-a half minute finished product was a highlight at the reception. They even spliced in Ryan's cell phone personalized message into the middle of it! We later made copies of this video for friends and included it in Ryan's web site.

My mom came down and my girlfriends took us out to lunch. We thought we needed to get out of the house. As we drove alone to lunch, my mom asked me what she could do to help me.

"I need you to make peace with my dad. Losing Ryan is bigger than your eighteen-year-old divorce and I saw you turn your head away when Dad arrived at the hospital. That hurts me. Please do this for me now." And they did. I consider it a gift from Ryan.

Then I had a very special visitor. The high school principal came to share with me and oh! How I appreciated her willingness to share. She, too, had lost a son although I didn't know that until that day. She came to offer me encouragement and it meant so much coming from a parent who had experienced this. Losing a child is called "the worst loss" anyone can face and there is a special bond between all parents who've lost a child. It's a club no one wants to belong to, but there is a bond in that club like no other.

Wednesday afternoon began the work party. All kinds of people came to hose and set up for Ryan's reception.

Bruce at Ryan's service:

As we would see the groups of kids arrive at our house, it was kind of fun, in a sad way. The older kids, Ryan's friends, would give us a hug and they were so articulate with their feelings. Graham's friends, the eighteen-year-olds, would walk in and eventually come up to us and say they were sorry. The sixteen-year-olds, Brady's friends, would sit on the couch but at some point, they'd say something. Dane's friends, the fourteen-year-olds, don't speak much like him, but they came. Their love was so heartfelt.

All Pam and I really wanted was a big backyard. We didn't really care about the house; we just wanted a place where our kids could hang out with all their friends.

I think we did a great job of that. We fed a lot of kids over the years. I talked to the accountant and tried to declare some of them as dependents but he didn't think it would fly. We have been so blessed, so very blessed and we wouldn't trade a minute of it.

I think it's common among parents to be pretty tough on our kids. When people would come up to us and say "We met your son, Ryan or Graham or Brady or Dane," our first reaction was often "Oh, oh... what did he do...he's dating your daughter" and so we'd hesitate until we hear what they had to say. But today, and this whole week, has really been a testament to Ryan and what a great kid he truly was.

I used to chide Ryan. You're going off to college now; it's time to make some new friends. But I want to say to you, Ryan's friends; you have the tightest bond of friendship we have ever seen. We want you to stay in our lives, to continue to be friends with our family.

We have this incredibly big backyard. It has been the site for Little League Dinner Dances, birthday parties, team parties, anniversary parties, and, we had hoped, perhaps a wedding reception. Now it would be the place for Ryan's memorial reception. People brought tables and chairs, centerpieces, trash cans etc. It was unbelievable how well Janet organized everything. She had people in charge of different groups; baseball, work, horses, neighbors etc. and each group was assigned a food item such as desserts or salad. Local businesses donated trays of food. Twenty pizzas arrived! It was a community effort. Someone brought forty rolls of toilet paper! Two dear friends picked up five hundred pounds of ice the day of the funeral and it was all organized into coolers to chill drinks. In the middle of this clean-up and set-up, more and more people kept coming by to express their sympathies to us. Somehow there was food and drinks for all those people as well!

One by one, in the middle of this effort to set up the back yard, I sent the boys upstairs to each write a good-bye letter to their brother.

Read by Candi at the service:

Dear Ryan,
How can I possibly start this off? I'm writing a goodbye letter to the only big brother that I'll ever have. You have been such an inspiration to us all. There have been so many

41

times when I wanted to give up and you wouldn't let me, when I wanted to turn back and you persuaded me to keep moving on. Every year at camp, the four of us huddle together on the last night and you tell us how proud you are of what we have become. I want you to know that I'm proud of you too, Ryan. There isn't another person in this world who was as loved by his peers, or as admired by his brothers. I know you will be watching over me from heaven until we are together again. I will never forget all of the wonderful times I got to spend with you. I love you with all my heart.

Graham, age 18

Dear Ryan,
Ever since I can remember, you have been my idol. I have always looked up to you as an example for everything in life. From what you wore to how you talked, you have been perfect in my mind. The thing that I have always admired most is your courage to face anything, and the way in which you faced your challenges. I am so glad that for the first time in three years we were able to live together again. I cannot imagine how devastating this ordeal would have been if you were still in Arizona. The example you have set for me all of my life has made me the strongest person I could possibly be. You have always shown me how to pull through the hardest times of my life.
Over the years at the Y.M.C.A. Camp Bluff Lake, watching how much your loving heart changes the lives of so many of your campers inspired me to try and follow your path and be a staff member, also. As I am becoming an adult and am finally on staff, my first instinct was to be in charge of the littlest kids and be your C.I.T. And when I felt that I had reached a maturity level to be able to take on the challenges of a rag, there was no doubt in my mind that you would be the one to tie my rag since you helped me reach that stage in

my life. Camp has always been a place in which our family has grown closer each year and I don't know how we will be able to spend a week there with you only in our hearts.

My life in general is not clear anymore, not only this horrible tragedy but also what direction this will lead me into. You have been the single person that has changed my life the most and it has been so tough to challenge each day without you. We have always been so close and the pain that we as a family feel is unspeakable. I love you so much and I feel empty without your gracious presence.

I love you and I miss you, Brady, age 16

Dear Ryan,

You have no idea what it was like to see your biggest brother and role model on his death bed. No one ever treated me with as much respect and dignity as you did. I have often been told by your friends how much you bragged about me. Your presence was always felt. You were so funny; you could always crack me up. I always loved just sitting down and talking to you about life because it was so easy and we could talk about anything. Your class and charm could not be matched. I had so much fun being your youngest brother. I will never forget all the great times we had at camp and on family trips. I love you, Ryan. The thought of you will always be inside of me.

Dane, age 14

It was Brady's expression "the pain we feel as a family is unspeakable" that played over and over in my head as I went to bed that evening.

Thursday, June 29th, 2000

When Ryan died, I told the boys, "Let's have this be the worst day of our lives. May nothing ever happen to us that is more devastating than this." On Thursday I said, "Let this be the saddest day of our lives." It was, but it was also so very beautiful.

Jim, Bruce's brother, at Ryan's service

It is with great sadness that I stand before you today to honor my beloved nephew, Ryan. I looked so forward to family gatherings to hear the latest adventures of Ryan. He would come up to me and wrap his arms around me in a hug, all 6'3" lanky Ryan. I will so miss those hugs. Losing Ryan has been the greatest tragedy of my life. He was my nephew, but, more importantly, he was my friend.

The five of us went together to the mortuary to see Ryan in the morning. We wanted some private time with him and we needed to make the final decision about opening the casket. The boys never asked us about the autopsy but Bruce and I were keenly aware that it might be too apparent. There is something so very final about seeing someone in a casket. There was a bandage on one finger that had been cut earlier in the week and it seemed so very out of place, and yet tender. We took some time to say goodbye again and went home.

Bruce and I still needed to write our goodbye letters to Ryan. Our plan was that Candi would read the letters from the boys, Bruce would read my letter and I would read his. Bruce so wanted to honor Ryan by speaking at his service, but he couldn't even speak when we were practicing in our bedroom. My sister would be the back up reader if Bruce couldn't do it. I honestly never thought I'd have to get up and speak that day but I kept remembering Bruce's dad's service nineteen months earlier. Bruce and I had sung and when I looked out in the church audience, I saw Ryan sitting in between Graham and Brady, with an arm around each brother, and tears rolling down his face. Afterwards, Ryan gave me one of his special hugs and told me how proud he was of us. We wanted Ryan to be proud of us again on this day and that's what I kept remembering. I knew that God and Ryan would be standing with us as we spoke, getting us through.

My letter to Ryan, read by Bruce

It is impossible to believe our adventure with you has come to an end. The agony we feel at losing you is a thousand times greater than any pain ever imagined.

You have always been so cherished, so very loved, (yes, even when you were being a "bugger"). I was in awe of the poise and confidence you possessed so very early. Thank you for being our son, our very best Christmas present. I will cherish my last conversation with you...as you rushed out the door, (late as usual) to the job you loved, you gave me one of your million dollar smiles and it took my breath away because you were so handsome.

Please do one last favor for me; will you lend me one of your smiles until we can find ours again?

Perhaps you talked so fast and embraced each day with such enthusiasm because you knew your time with us was short. You will always be in our hearts as we know Jesus holds you in his arms now. We are so proud of the man you had become.

I love you so very much, Mom

As much as I remember details of everything that happened, I know that I was in shock. As we were getting ready to leave for the service, a good friend arrived at our house with food and hugged me. I had no idea who he was! I'm sorry, Joe!

Tim and Shelley came to drive us to the church with April. All our other family and friends would meet us there. We couldn't imagine a sadder destination than going to our son's funeral service. Our family had always been so joyous and how I wanted that spirit of joy back, that family back. We had always relied on humor and so we told jokes to lighten our heavy hearts on this short drive to the church.

And then we were there. Everyone was there. We had agreed to wait in a different room and not greet people then. It felt surreal. Bruce left the family room for a short time and graciously thanked people for coming. We decided to walk down the aisle of the church together, the five of us, April, grandparents, aunts, uncles, cousins, Tim and Shelley to begin this service. The church held nine hundred people seated but there were people everywhere. People were standing in the narthex and also outside the church only to be able to hear the service. The best guesstimate is that twelve hundred friends and family came to support us and to honor Ryan. We thank all of you.

As we walked down the aisle, I remember thinking how beautiful it was. The stained glass windows were spectacularly colorful and the sunlight streaming through the glass was shining on Ryan's coffin, picking up the colors of his flowers. I had ordered flowers that would be bright like Ryan, never realizing until I saw it all together, that it matched the church windows. It was so beautiful; it was like a wedding, the wedding he'd never have.

Everything I have read since, talks about the regrets parents often experience about their child's service. We have no regrets. It was everything we wanted it to be. Jim, Ron Clear and Candi all eulogized Ryan with such thoughtfulness, they captured his spirit. And then it was Bruce's turn.

"I don't know if I can do this so bear with me." And then he began to read Katie O'Connor's letter and when he got to the part where he read "after knowing him, it was impossible not to aspire to be like him. So many people want to be the friend that Ryan was" Bruce became Bruce. I could see it happen. He relaxed, he spoke from his heart, he even joked a little, and he was Ryan's father...raw, broken but still strong, compassionate and tender. I could see the change come over him and I knew he'd get through, so I knew I would also. Before Bruce read my letter, I joined him. I walked right up to the microphone and read Bruce's letter without ever really looking at the sea of faces before me. I made it until almost the end before breaking down.

Bruce's letter to Ryan, read by me

Dear Ryan,

As a father, I couldn't have asked for a finer son than you. I am so proud of the young man you have become. I tried to teach you values and life skills you would need on your journey to adulthood. I wanted you to be caring and sensitive, you were. I wanted you to respect women, you did. I wanted you to be friendly and kind, you were. I wanted to teach you sports. You far exceeded my expectations, the natural athlete in so many ways. The years we spent in Little League together, NJB Basketball and soccer will give us all memories forever. You became such an accomplished skier and snowboarder and soon surpassed me. What great times we had as a family together. I wanted you to learn to use your hands and be able to fix things. Soon you were taking apart everything—skateboards, bikes, jet skis, cars. I wanted you to be ambitious, you were. It was so exciting to see your enthusiasm for your job this summer and your desire to do well in school.

Ryan, you're the best big brother to Graham, Brady and Dane that we could have ever hoped for. They wanted to please you, dress like you, and be like you in every way. We will miss you greatly but are so thankful for the twenty-one years we had together.

I love you, Dad

We both believe that Ryan and God helped us to speak. We sat down holding hands and I could again see Ryan's face after his grandfather's funeral, "Mom, I have never been so proud of you."

Bob Pietsch offering reassurance.

I've not had an opportunity to get to know this family for very long and I feel very privileged to be a part of this sacred moment....your love, your willingness to share from your hearts...and I do express my appreciation for that.

I think of all of you young people who are here today. I know that if I were you, and it's a question I, myself, have asked many times, because I, too, lost a son, at age 27, and the first question I asked was "Why, Why, Why?" It seems so ill timed, I don't understand. I'm baffled. Why death itself? But we know for certain that that time will come for all of us, whether sooner or later. It seems so incongruous and yet, I believe, and this is what I have tried to live by in subsequent years, the question isn't 'Why?," the question is 'What?' What is really important? What really matters at a moment like this? Not things, not degrees, not status, none of that is really important at times like this. It all comes down to one word...relationships. Look at you here! Loved ones, friends, here to support, not knowing what to say...to have friends like that is overwhelming and this family has expressed that overwhelming sense again and again. Hold onto those relationships. Relationships to friends, to family. This family of yours, I've not gotten to know very well but I see qualities I really like. In this day and age, when there is so much brokenness, in times of crisis, to really feel that sense of love and support....

There is one other relationship that is often forgotten in times of prosperity, and that is the relationship to God. We are created to live in a relationship with God, to really know him. I think of the fact that Ryan was born on Christmas Day...what a day! That day was the announcement that God had come to live with us, Emanuel.

What is really important? Relationships, friends, family and the family of God.

Bob Pietsch invited everyone back to our house for the reception following a brief graveside service. We were the last to leave the church and went to Ryan's coffin one last time to say goodbye before we closed it. We put our goodbye letters next to him and then came the tortuous moment of closing the coffin. How I hated to close it! Even though I knew, and believed, that Ryan was in heaven with God and Jesus, I just didn't want to leave his physical body.

The cemetery is just a short distance from the church and we planned to have a brief prayer and song there only. Some things, however, are not going to be any different, even in tragic circumstances. Bruce's mom and her companion were not anywhere to be found and we waited and waited for them. Bruce announced that perhaps she was walking her dog but still, she did not come. Finally arriving, she said she'd been visiting with friends at church, and so we could finally begin. Bob Pietsch said a prayer and a blessing. A bagpiper played "Amazing Grace" while we tried to sing along but it was hard to hear him so Bruce and I led everyone in "Amazing Grace" again, a capella. Bruce got his wish, we sang.

We wanted the reception at our house to be a celebration of Ryan's life and it was. Ryan's friends had decorated his truck with a wreath and flowers and left it parked in front of our home. Parking was a nightmare but everyone worked together and we celebrated until the wee hours of the morning. Close friends of Ryan's, and some not as close, secretly confided that they'd hoped we'd be their in-laws one day. Ryan's friends presented us with a wheel beautifully arranged in a basket of plants and flowers. The card read, "In our circle of friends, RYAN is now the missing spoke. We will treasure our memories of him and remember him always."

As the sun faded on that hot day, we viewed Ryan's video twice! With Janet's incredible Funeral Franc organizational skills, there was food and drink for everyone but we did eventually run out of toilet paper even though we started out with forty rolls!

Ryan..... Thursday, June 29, 2000

And when the party's over the guests have all gone home and all that's left are memories how loud they'll linger on

The rooms they seem to echo the walls they scream his name the pictures say he's still alive his death was just a wasted game

and yet, a star shines brightly in the dark and blackened sky it is our star, named Ryan shining down from oh so high

His life on earth was finished and a bright star he became just look up to the heavens and you'll hear them call his name

He watches and he comforts us from heaven up above for though his life on earth is over his star shines bright with love

God knew what he was doing though he took him from our reach for Ryan's now immortal

His memories we all will keep

Ryan is with all of us now at all times, God bless you today, May he hold you and comfort you And may you know that all of us share your pain and loss this day—

Debbie Milovic

Blessings

The day after Ryan's funeral, my nephew, Travis, asked me why I wasn't angry with God. I never have been. I believe that God gave me the greatest hope and comfort in my lowest times. I believe, with all my heart, that Ryan is in heaven and that I will be with him again when I die. I cannot imagine losing a child without faith. I don't know what hope you would have. I never believed that God did this to us. I have never believed that God worked that way. I don't believe that we were chosen to experience this tragedy because of something we did or didn't do. I never thought this was "of" God's hand, but I could see God's hand in it helping us through. I could see this from the very beginning.

My journal entry, July 9, 2000

Things I am grateful for...

1. *We were all there when Ryan died—the five of us, all grandparents, Candi, Taylor, Travis, Sharie, April, Jim, Susan. Carter had been there first and was alone with Ryan when he arrived at Loma Linda Hospital. All the grandparents travel a great deal. My mom and Art had just returned from a five week trip. What*

if they'd been in Europe and were unreachable? Dane plays competitive travel baseball and had been in Omaha, Nebraska two weeks earlier. He had been in Washington D.C. until June 23rd with his eighth grade class. What if we'd had to fly this fourteen-year-old home alone because his brother died?

2. *Loma Linda is a wonderful hospital…well respected. Ryan got great care.*
3. *Ryan didn't die at San Gorgonio, the first hospital. It helped us to process what was happening to him and to be a part of it. If Ryan had died at San Gorgonio, it would have been even more unbelievable.*
4. *We didn't have to make any decisions to turn off machines. We probably would have wanted to hold onto any slice of Ryan and how he would have hated that. I think Ryan died to spare us any difficult decisions.*
5. *He wasn't in any pain. After Ryan collapsed, he never felt anything again.*
6. *Ryan didn't did do anything stupid or dangerous. No one did anything stupid or dangerous to him. No one else was hurt. It just happened. We have been spared so much.*
7. *I am grateful for my faith. I don't know how you could survive losing a child without faith.*
8. *Ryan believed. He is now in heaven.*

I learned to continue adding blessings to this list as the year progressed. One of the most important blessings has been Graham, Brady and Dane's ability to empathize on a very real, deep level with the pain of other people. I consider this to be a true blessing.

He Said Goodbye

I came to believe in the weeks following Ryan's death that he said goodbye to people. It was as if, on some level, he knew he was going to die. There are too many stories and too many random reconnections for me to believe that this is all coincidence. It was as if Ryan was reaching out, one last time, to touch the lives of those who loved him.

A friend of a friend had been killed earlier in the week. Ryan had told me about Zach's death and, although he barely knew him, he was very moved by his passing. My last conversation with Ryan was on Friday morning, June 23rd, as he was rushing out the door, late as usual, to work and I was leaving for Santa Barbara. Ryan said, "You know, Mom, we're not all going to make it to our fifth reunion from high school. How weird is that?'

"You're right. You just have to cherish each day and be wise."

"Mom, I do. You don't ever have to worry about me. I love you."

Bruce had had a similar conversation with Ryan about Zach's passing.

Josh was with Ryan when he collapsed and lost consciousness. The last thing Ryan said to Josh, to anyone, was "I love you, Buddy."

Ryan hadn't been living in California for a year because he was attending the University of Arizona in Tucson. He'd been home since mid-May and reconnected with so many high school friends. Allison had a chance to make amends to Ryan and others also spent time with him. Another friend had had friends over on Friday, June 23rd, and talked with Ryan about how precious these high school friendships continued to be. Friends that were there at her house shared that Ryan had been unusually reflective that night.

Sam, a friend and roommate at the University of Arizona, met Ryan in San Clemente for lunch before leaving on a summer vacation. As Ryan left the parking lot, he rolled down the window of his truck and blew Sam a kiss. Sam thought it was a weird thing for Ryan to do, out of character for him. Sam later told me that this was the first thing he thought about when he'd heard that Ryan died.

Ryan, I want you to know that I haven't worried about you since you died. I know you're fine. I know you're in heaven. I just worry about us.

At the Hospital

1. Ask questions. The nurses and social workers are a wonderful resource. They both can explain again medical procedures and what to expect. They are there to help you.
2. Ask for a chaplain if you'd like. Most hospitals also have chapels where you can go to pray.
3. Friends and family that go to the hospital should bring food, drinks, aspirin, pillows and blankets if possible. The immediate family members often have not left their loved one's side, and don't want to go anywhere to eat. The hospital can't dispense even an aspirin to non-patients and yet it's common to experience headaches during such a difficult time.
4. If possible, ask the family if there is anything you can bring to them from home. Contact lens wearers may want their glasses. I am near-sighted and wear disposable lenses. At the hospital I eventually threw away my contacts because they were so clouded from my tears. I didn't have my glasses with me.
5. We were so very grateful that we knew Ryan's wishes to be an organ donor. Ryan had indicated on his license that he wanted to be a donor but his friends had his wallet and so the hospital never saw his license. It's so important to

have had this discussion with your loved ones because, even if you have indicated your wishes on your driver's license or on a legal document, the family often makes the final decision. At a time of tremendous sadness, it can be very helpful to the grieving family to know that something good will come out of tragedy. The need for organ donation is much publicized. A single donor's organs could save the lives of as many as eight people. However, as was true in Ryan's case, organs are not always viable. Tissue donation is much less publicized but, I have now learned, one donation can help thirty to forty people. Corneas can restore sight. Heart valves are used on both adults and children. Skin is used for burn victims and can be stored for up to eighteen months. Veins, bone segments and soft tissue are used by cardiac, orthopedic, plastic and neurological surgeons. It is important to know that organ and tissue donation does not prevent the family from having an open casket, nor does it delay the funeral. There is no cost to the family. All costs related to donation are paid by the recipients and their health insurance. Friends and family who are supporting the grieving family might suggest tissue donation as an alternative to organ donation, if the organs are not viable.

6. Ask the nurses to clip a lock of your loved one's hair.

Small Tips for the Grieving

1. Find a location for the service first. Everything else will fall into place around that.
2. Take the social security number of your loved one with you to the mortuary. It is needed for the death certificate and for official notifications.
3. You will need more than one copy of the death certificate. The mortuary will order these for you. Depending upon the age of your loved one, the mortician will advise you on how many death certificates you will need. You will need an original death certificate to close bank accounts or to change a pink slip on a car. Airlines will accept a copy of a death certificate to grant a bereavement fare to family members flying in for the funeral. We didn't receive Ryan's death certificates until November and so one of my nephews wasn't able to reconcile his airline fare until then.
4. Most mortuaries and cemeteries have payment plans available and can help you make those arrangements. They will also advise you if your loved one is eligible for benefits. Anyone receiving Medicaid would be eligible for help from the Department of Social Services. Military service may also mean eligibility for burial in a Veterans' cemetery.

5. There are coffins available on the internet with overnight shipping. Many mortuaries will match these prices. Friends might help you research this before you go to the mortuary.

6. Wait to order the headstone. It's the most visible, permanent decision you make at a time when no one can be making good decisions. As you get more comfortable, walk around the cemetery. You'll be inspired by headstones you see and then come up with a good idea for one. Anyone who has been in the military may be eligible for a headstone provided by the U.S. government. The cemetery can advise you on that.

7. Wear small earrings and comfortable shoes. Grief is exhausting in itself. Hugging is especially tiring because people hold you a long time trying to comfort you. My ears were bleeding after the first few days from earrings digging into my earlobes when people were hugging me.

8. Clinique waterproof mascara does not run.

9. Talk to your doctor about possibly prescribing some medication for a short time if you can't sleep or if you find you can't function. Be responsible with this medication. Check with your doctor about the combination of alcohol and medication. Alcohol often is not recommended and may interfere with sleep.

10. Have a guest book for people to sign at the service.

11. Let your friends and family take care of you. It will help you to have them there and it will help them to have something to do.

12. Journal. I journal in complete sentences but that is my style. There is no "right was to journal. I kept a journal for six months. It was very cathartic to write down my feelings.

Small Tips for Friends and Family of the Grieving

1. Be there. Even if it scares you and you don't know what to say. Be there, at the house, at the funeral. Help.
2. Bring basic supplies such as toilet paper, soap and milk. No one is going to the market and yet supplies do run short. Bring paper supplies.

3. Do the laundry and the dishes.
1. Instead of saying, "Call me if you need anything," check in with the grieving family or the one organizing the reception.
2. Make lists of phone calls, flowers and food. Mark the food clearly that you put in the freezer with labels that identify the food and baking instructions. One time, we ate dessert for dinner. We ate mystery funeral casserole for several months because we would have no idea what it was until it was thawed and cooked.
3. Write a personal note on a card or flowers and sign your last name. Your friends may very well know who Mike and Kim are in normal circumstances but, in a time like this, they may find that they know several "Mikes and Kims."

4. Write again at three months and around the first anniversary. It will mean everything to the grieving family if you continue to remember. Some people sent us several cards and letters and we appreciated it so very much. Even if you just simply say, "I'm still thinking about you" or "I still remember." Say this when you run into someone who has lost someone recently.

5. Sign the guest book at the service. The grieving may be overwhelmed by the number of people there but it will mean a lot to them to know you were there.

6. Don't say that you know exactly how someone feels unless you've lost someone in the same relationship. I found myself comforting other people who told me they knew exactly how I felt because they'd lost their mother or their dog and then they'd collapse in my arms!

7. Don't say "You'll never get over this." I was in such, raw pain when Ryan died and this comment scared me. What if I felt like this the rest of my life? It was impossible to hear this, in the beginning, as anything but an overwhelming prediction.

8. Don't tell a grieving person "It's time to get over this." Grief is a process and it takes a long, long time. Instead of someone hearing your concern, he just might stop sharing with you. If you feel that someone close to you is stuck in this process, approach it very gently, with care and concern.

9. Write down fond memories and funny stories about the person who died. These will be cherished by the family.

10. Take pictures to be duplicated. We were so grateful to live in a time when computer scanning made it possible to duplicate photographs without a negative. Friends collected pictures in a basket for us during that first week and I was able to select favorite ones and get copies of my own. Some of Ryan's friends made copies of their own pictures and brought them to us.

14. If you are at the cemetery, go visit the grave and then tell your friend you were there. It meant so much to us that friends and family visited Ryan's grave. We eventually made a "mailbox" with a freezer bag and clothes pins so kids could leave letters there and we left inspirational poems for visitors to read.

1. Go with the grieving one to visit the grave. I was recently at the cemetery for someone else's graveside service and Ryan was buried nearby. Someone asked me where Ryan was buried and then walked with me to see his headstone. It was such a thoughtful gesture and I really appreciated it.

2. If the family establishes a foundation in memory of their loved one, make a contribution. The donations to Ryan's foundation, no matter how much or how little, meant the world to us. There are many charities that may be meaningful. Help the family with ideas to honor their loved one.

Thanking People

We appreciated deeply the love and support we received since Ryan's passing. The overwhelming task of thanking people needed to be tackled. But how do you begin? I decided that I'd have two notes printed and I came to call them, "The Casserole and Prayer note" and "The Foundation note." Some people received both. I wrote personal notes to many people. We duplicated copies of Ryan's video for some of our friends, family and Ryan's friends. One of our beginning adjustments was signing everyone's name but Ryan's. This was so very difficult.

Dearest Friends,

We are completely overwhelmed by the tremendous outpouring of love we have received since Ryan's passing. At a time when our family needed support, you were there with food, prayer, a visit, flowers, plants, a note and help. Please accept our most heartfelt thanks and know that we will always remember your comforting expression of sympathy.

With deep gratitude, Bruce and Pam Ferguson Graham, Brady and Dane

The Ryan Ferguson Foundation

Thank you for your generous contribution to the Ryan Ferguson Foundation. We would like Ryan's love of life, his love of sport and his beautiful spirit to live on so that young people can continue to be touched by Ryan. Two of the experiences that Ryan enjoyed sharing most with his family and friends were counseling campers and playing baseball. Through your support, we have established a perpetual scholarship fund for the Orange Y.M.C.A. Camp Bluff Lake and the Villa Park High School Baseball Program. Your kindness, love and prayers are so very appreciated.

Fondly, Bruce and Pam Ferguson Graham, Brady and Dane
www.ryanfergusonfoundation.com

Zestfully

Jeff Wagner, at Ryan's service:

*R*yan *was born on Christmas Day and his mom said he was the best Christmas gift they'd ever received. Ryan was a gift to all of our lives and God said that every good and perfect gift comes from him. Life is a gift. Every moment, every breath you take, is a gift from God. And Ryan took on life heads first, with energy, passion, enthusiasm, even for the smallest things. He lived life to its fullest. Life is a gift meant to be lived like that.*

What a legacy Ryan has left! He lived his life joyfully, making every moment memorable. He helped people look at the brighter side of things. He took risks. Wherever Ryan went, adventure was sure to follow. He was famous for his smile. He zestfully loved life, his friends and his family.

Letter by Lauren O'Connor. She felt he
had said good-bye.

Ryan's strong family ties were apparent to everyone who knew him. As a family, you raised him to be a funny, friendly man with a gleaming, magnetic personality and unique charisma and confidence. Over the years, the sound of his familiar voice became part of the landscape of our tight cir-cle of friends, all of whom cherished his characteristic gestures and facial expressions as much during his lifetime as we do now in reflection.

Ryan holds a special place in all of our hearts.

A couple of weeks ago, I saw him for the first time since we celebrated the millennium in Lake Tahoe. He and I rang in the New Year with a friendly kiss, a memory that will be engraved in my mind forever. Ryan had the ability to make every minute memorable. I absolutely adored having him for a friend.

Brandon Joffe's letter on taking risks was read by
Bruce at Ryan's service

In remembering all of our adventures and experiences together, I realized what an effect Ryan had on me as a child. I realized that there is one thing I learned from him as a child that was vital in the building of who I am today. You see Ryan was born almost without fear. I was born more timid and cautious. Ryan many times forced me to push away fear and to push limits that I alone never would have pushed. He was always ready to lead me and the other kids in the neighborhood into activities and events that seemed impossible, and often incredibly scary. With Ryan, there were almost no limits. He could jump from any roof or tree and not be touched. I learned to take risks in being with him. I think that my experiences with him helped me to realize that a big part of living is facing fear. Ryan knew how to face fear and live life to the fullest. Ryan lived more in his young childhood than many adults have lived in their whole lives. I'll never forget him.

Jean Gorgie wrote to us about Ryan the camper
and the role model:

*I met Ryan at Camp Bluff Lake when he was about nine,
and I was around eighteen. He was at archery and not hit-
ting much but the dirt. When it was time for him to go around
the rail to pick up his arrows, he instead tried to bend over
the front guard rail to reach those that were on the ground.
I watched this hysterical spectacle as his long, skinny arms
and legs flailed about while he tried to keep from landing
head first into the dirt. At one point, he looked over at me
and gave me a huge smile. He then proceeded to flip over the
railing and land with a thump on his back. He got up, dusted
himself off and gave me another "Ryan" grin. For years
afterward, I called him the "arrow boy." Looking back, I
know that he was trying to make me laugh, and he certainly
did. Every summer since then, I have looked forward to just
being around Ryan.*

*As a counselor, Ryan was a great role model. He often
was given the youngest (the toughest) cabin and his energy
and patience were amazing. I cannot tell you how many
times I've looked over to see him at the center of this seeming
chaos; knee-high in kids swirled around him, and wanting to
get his attention, they all talked at the same time. I'd catch
his eye, and again he would give me a dazzling Ryan smile. I
know that he made a positive impact on the life of each child
he encountered. Years from now, they will look back on their
childhood and when they remember the joy of being a child,
they will remember Ryan. He will be the one who gave them
those childhood memories which are so precious and which
will be carried in the heart and told to future generations.*

Alexis Moran also wrote about Ryan, the joyous
camp counselor:

*Every year I found it fascinating to see which one of
the male counselors would wind up with the littlest boys'
cabin and to see how well they could "handle" them. It just
so happened that Ryan got them last year. I was down at
Lakefront during free period with my cabin playing volley-
ball. Ryan was there with a bunch of male counselors. The
little boys must have been with their co-counselor because
he was without them until about five minutes later, when all
of the sudden, I heard this loud roar of child-like voices and
I turned around to see a giant dust cloud rising and getting
closer. The cloud died down and a whole hoard of dirty little
boys jumped onto any free space of Ryan's body. He got up
and was just dripping with little boys. I mean he had two on
his neck, one on his back, two on each arm, and about six or
seven at various places at his legs.*

*But that was not the part I remember the most….it was
his reaction to this. He had the biggest smile on his face,
it was as if he was expecting it, but he looked so happy. I
remember this moment. It was the clincher of what definitely
made me want to be with children and work at the Y. It was
the sheer look of pure joy on his face and that smile, the Ferg
family smile. I knew that this was life at the simplest of joys.*

The letters we received sharing stories about Ryan at
camp are especially important to us because we didn't get
to see Ryan, the counselor, in action. I did witness Ryan getting off the bus after a week at camp when one of his little
guys tripped and fell. Ryan scooped him up in his arms and
tenderly comforted him. What I saw then, was that Ryan was
mirroring his own dad. He was a father to these little guys
for one week.

Ryan lived his life to the fullest and loved deeply. He felt that he and Natalie were soul mates. Lorrie Walk, Natalie's mom wrote of this love and what he had meant to her family:

I cannot express in appropriate words what Ryan meant to my family. The loss my daughter feels shall remain with her forever, as she truly loved Ryan and cannot imagine life without him. If only we all could have just one more day, just one more moment to spend with him, just to say goodbye.

I was always so happy to see Ryan when he would come to visit Natalie. He brought joy to all of us. He befriended my youngest daughter, Steffanie, at a most difficult period in her life. He even became a moderator at times, when Natalie and Steffanie were ready to attack each other, as siblings often do. I loved to hear his tales of Camp Bluff Lake after he would return each summer from his sessions. Ryan told me he would do this every year, even into his forties. I was so impressed with his motivation and enthusiasm in this endeavor. In fact, Ryan never ceased to intrigue me with his vibrant enthusiasm for any new venture he may have been undertaking. We were so sad when he left for Tucson, but knew this was the right move for him. On his frequent visits, he would be so excited about his future and had such great plans. This world is a lesser place without him, for he had so much to contribute to so many lives.

You both are simply amazing in your grace, manner and hospitality while under such duress. I am in awe of your ability to orchestrate such a magnificent and deserving tribute to your son. As parents, you raised a wonderful young man with qualities so admirable. There is no loss greater than that of losing a child. My heart breaks for you, but I can only imagine the pain and grief you must be feeling. We loved Ryan so much and shall remember him always.

All of these letters are such a gift to us. We have boxes and boxes of the letters and cards sent and sometimes, I take them out to read them again. These words of comfort are not only blessings to us, but they have allowed us to see Ryan as others saw him. Through these communications, I learned so much about Ryan and I have never been more proud of him.

My journal entry, July 19th, 2000

I continue to be so very touched by Ryan's friends and their willingness to share what he meant to them. I have never been prouder of Ryan.

Bruce and I have talked a lot about saying goodbye to Ryan. We both deeply appreciate being with him when he died and count it as a blessing. But, neither one of us has a feeling that we didn't get to say goodbye to him. We have always told our boys how loved they were and how much they meant to us. We don't feel there was anything left unsaid to Ryan. In those first few days after Ryan's passing, Bruce said to me, "I was there. I was at his games and I coached him, We spent a lot of time together and took great family vacations. I have no regrets other than that he's not here now." How many fathers could say that?

To be remembered for your smile; joyful spirit; zestful appreciation of life; leadership and passionate connection to people is the way we should all want to be remembered. This is how we remember Ryan.

Letter from Annie and Jim Hughes:
June 30, 2000

Yesterday was a celebration of Ryan's vitality, energy and accomplishments. In his time with you, he became all a parent or a brother could hope for. His legacy will be remembered through the Ryan Ferguson Foundation—how wonderful!

I just wanted to share with you a story that brought me great comfort when I was experiencing an unbearable loss a few years ago (and you were there for us): "Our lives are like a tapestry viewed from the backside where there's just a bunch of knotted threads that are criss-crossed and tangled with no apparent plan or design. And only when our grief and anger and pain have subsided, can we see that the tapestry is an intricate and beautiful rendering of our life with all the twists and turns it takes to make us the person we become."

Small Things and Incredible Gestures that really helped

1. The church gave us an audio tape of Ryan's service and I treasure it. I sometimes listen to it in my car and I find it very comforting.
2. Our friends kept inviting us to dinner. They surrounded us in love and companionship and let us talk.
3. People wrote to us several times. Some families sent us letters from each member of their family telling what Ryan had meant to them. Some neighbors that we had never met wrote to us expressing their sympathy.
4. Graham was supposed to have left for Hawaii the day before the funeral for his senior trip. All his friends decided they wanted to be here for Graham and didn't want to go on the trip without him so they postponed the trip a month.
5. The high school baseball team canceled practice so all the players could attend the funeral.
6. Some local businesses closed for the funeral so people could attend...
7. The marquis at the high school read "V.P.H.S. remembers Ryan Ferguson" all summer.

8. A friend had a silver charm bracelet made for me with Ryan's initials on it that I wear daily.

9. Another friend had a bouquet of twenty-one silk teardropped roses made for my living room in the perfect colors with an engraved silver tag of Ryan's initials and his years. They match perfectly.

10. A childhood friend of Ryan's took the time to copy her diary pages from seventh grade and brought them to us. "I'm in love with a left-handed pitcher named Ferg......" It was so very sweet.

11. One family dedicated their Christmas card to Ryan's memory.

12. A family member got us on the mailing list for "The Compassionate Friends," a newsletter for parents who've lost a child. The publication comes monthly and it has been very helpful and appreciated. Reading it helps to normalize what I'm feeling.

13. People left us messages on our voice mail to let us know they were thinking about us.

14. We had a year of family grief counseling with a dear colleague, Dr. Kim Storm.

15. A friend I hadn't seen in years went with me to the cemetery the first time I bought Ryan flowers. She has visited with me several times.

16. Camp Bluff Lake had a memorial campfire and dedicated the chapel there to Ryan.

17. The Villa Park High School Baseball team dedicated the season to Ryan and wore his number on their sleeves. A monument was built at the high school field to honor Ryan. The team also had a throw blanket made for us with this monogrammed on it.

18. For Mother's Day, a girlfriend had an original watercolor made for me.

19. This same sweet friend helped me decorate Ryan's grave for the first anniversary.

20. A psychologist and editor, donated her time, and met with me to work on the manuscript.

Gender Grieving and What
I Learned to Say

I am blessed to be married to a man who can really express his feelings and is not afraid to do so. We have always been very, very close. We have always been able to talk. I knew how deeply Bruce grieved Ryan and our ability to discuss it together has been the foundation of our surviving this loss. Some statistics place the divorce rate for couples who have lost a child as high as 80%. I think that is often because one person needs to talk and the other one finds talking way too painful. We talked and talked and still do. We still cry together often. We started walking daily and this gave us an hour to talk uninterrupted. We still do this. What surprised me was that while just about everyone let me talk, few men were comfortable enough to let Bruce talk.

In the beginning, I almost could not distinguish between Bruce's grief and mine. When girlfriends would ask me how he was doing, I would talk about how it was for both of us, as if our experience was exactly the same. It pretty much was the same. We were both so very heartbroken and we were both determined to find a way to be gracious and strong in the face of this unspeakable pain.

We knew that grieving parents often become bitter and angry. Some tried to drown their pain in alcohol. As a therapist, I have always learned from my patients and children who had lost siblings often told me how forgotten they felt by their grieving parents. They described months of begging their parents to eat or their mom isolating herself in bed. They understood that their parents were in pain but they were too! We knew our boys needed us, and we needed them, too! We understood that we had choices to make and those choices would dramatically effect our boys. It seemed to us to almost be a question of character. We couldn't change or control what had happened, but we could control how we handled it. We could choose to fall apart and make the boys give up their lives to take care of us or we could find a way to survive that would be meaningful. We felt that we would dishonor Ryan's legacy if we behaved in an isolating, self-pitying manner. We also knew that the boys would follow our lead. If we became bitter or angry at God, then they would be, too. We needed our faith. The belief that we would be together again with Ryan has always been comforting.

I knew, as a therapist, that siblings didn't like to be "forced" to go to the cemetery. We felt lucky that the cemetery was so close so the boys could go when they wanted to go. Sometimes, we took Dane with us and he would tenderly wrap an arm around us, trying to comfort his grieving parents.

We both made a commitment to be strong. That never meant that we wouldn't be sad, or cry, or heartbroken; it simply meant that our grief wouldn't destroy us or our family. We didn't want Ryan's death to be the end of our family. We were still a family of six; one of us now lived in heaven.

There were some differences in our reactions. I needed to talk to Bruce a lot about the scenes in the hospital and he hated how often I wanted to discuss it. He didn't want to remember the horror of the hospital and I couldn't stop the images from playing over and over again in my head. This "instant replay" went on for months.

My journal entry on July 8, 2000

Bruce doesn't remember all the blood at the end as Ryan's chest was heaving and his hand was jerking. He was watching the monitors go flat. But I find strange comfort in remembering all the blood because it tells me he never would have been okay and I know Ryan would have just hated that.

I wanted to read everything I could about grief and loss. I was especially interested in books written for grieving parents. We were given a whole series of books which Bruce dubbed my "Life Sucks but God is Good" series. Bruce didn't want to read anything at all and relied on me to share relevant information.

Bruce had "survivor's guilt." Why did he get to travel and do things when Ryan didn't? Why had he been given a longer life? This seemed more gender related. I didn't experience much "survivor's guilt" during this journey of grief.

Bruce was worried that something would happen to one of the other boys but I was convinced that we had paid the greatest price and nothing would ever happen to one of us again. I felt like we could drive the wrong way down a one way street and we'd probably still be okay. It took me awhile to accept that there is no such thing as "being safe from tragedy." Graham told us after the funeral, "Let's make a pact to never be the front row at a funeral again." I wish we could promise that to the boys.

We recognized that we were all anxious. The unthinkable had happened. Things don't always turn out okay. I had always believed that bad news would find you and that had certainly been true with Ryan. Bruce and I agreed that we would not become overprotective of the other boys. Ryan didn't die because he was being careless or reckless. He just died. It seemed to us that it would dishonor him by changing the rules on things we let Graham, Brady and Dane do. When people ask us how we can let the other boys take risks like Snowboarding, this is what we explain to them. Perhaps we would have reacted differently if Ryan's tragic death had been caused by carelessness. We have agreed, as a family, to really keep in touch with one another. I find that the boys check in with us more.

Bruce and I also agreed that we would not allow the boys to use their brother's death as an excuse for their behavior. In the first few days, we told them that they'd had about a week to tell a police officer that they were speeding because their brother had died and that time was almost up. Our expectations for them were not going to change. We were not going to let the boys become victims of their brother's death and the boys have met our standards.

Bruce and I were puzzled at how uncomfortable some people, especially men, seemed to be with grief. Three months after Ryan died; Bruce went on a five-day horseback ride with a group of men who had been going on this ride together for years. Almost no one mentioned Ryan's death to Bruce and he came home bewildered that men are so out of touch with their feelings! It was as if Bruce's pain might touch them and so men wouldn't ask. Instead, men would ask Bruce how I was doing or how the boys were doing. Bruce would often ask me, "When did men decide crying wasn't okay? Where did that come from?" Grief makes some people uncomfortable because it makes them feel helpless so they will comment "You're doing better" when the visible signs of grief are less apparent.

People expected Bruce to be back at work. That was somehow a measure of how well he was doing. If Bruce could work, he must be handling his grief okay. Bruce did not receive any negative comments about returning to work.

He runs a company and returned to work the week after the funeral. He would come home very early each day, around 3:00, and we would together go to the cemetery. We would take, each day, bouquets of flowers from our house and leave them on the graves of other people we knew who were buried there. That first week after the funeral, this became a daily ritual. It provided a way for us to get comfortable with the cemetery and a way to begin again with our lives.

When Bruce had been back to work a few weeks, he had a sales meeting. Most of his employees are single or don't have children, and so, even though they knew Ryan, Bruce hadn't known how their reaction would be to this devastating loss and he was concerned they wouldn't understand his pain. He told me that during the sales meeting, he thanked everyone for their overwhelming support since Ryan's passing. He looked down and saw drops of water on the conference table. He hadn't realized until that moment, that he was crying!

Apparently, that same standard about returning to work was not applied to me and most of the critical comments were from women! "If I had lost a child, I could never return to work."

This was one of those challenging comments where I felt I was expected to interpret it and then be gracious. I think this was meant to be a compliment, as in, "I don't think I could be as strong as you are being and return to work." Instead of the way it could be heard, "I must love my child more than you loved your deceased son since I'd never go back to work."

With practice, I learned to reply to these comments. "Ryan cherished his relationships and since I am in the business of helping people improve their relationships, I believe I honor his memory by continuing my work."

I felt protective of my patients. Their therapy could not be about my loss and yet some had heard when I returned to work. On my very first day back to work, I received a phone call from a colleague. He asked me how I was doing and I assumed he knew about Ryan. He didn't and hesitated then to tell me the real reason for his call. Someone very close to his adult-age son had committed suicide and he wanted to know if I'd see his son. I wasn't sure I was ready to help anyone else through a tragic death, but, as I thought about it more, I knew that I could. I felt Ryan's gentle push to go forward with my work, work that I had always found so fulfilling. I imagined another therapist helping one of Ryan's friends. It seemed that over the course of those first few months, I helped a lot of people deal with grief and loss.

I still work to find a balance on telling my patients about Ryan. Some do know and some will never know. I have learned to answer direct questions about my sons in careful ways. "How old is your oldest son?"

"Christmas Day is his twenty-third birthday."

Bruce carries his family photographs in a different part of his wallet than I do. I have a great picture of all four boys next to my driver's license and so people see it when they are checking my identification. I learned how to respond to reactions of the photograph in a way that protected others and me. "This picture was taken when the boys were thirteen, fifteen, seventeen and twenty. The youngest is fifteen now." We both tell people that we have four boys when asked how many children we have. Sometimes we add that the youngest two still live at home. The boys each also answer that they have three brothers. Bruce and I still refer to them as our second, third and youngest sons. This has always been how we described our family and that hasn't changed. We are still working on what to say to people. It's a process.

And There Were Signs

Before Ryan died, I probably would have said that I didn't believe in signs. However, I believe that Ryan has sent us so many messages of reassurance. Finding his copy of "Footprints" on our way to make the arrangements at the mortuary was the first sign. I keep my eyes wide open now because I know I've missed some!

My birthday is July 1st, two days after Ryan's funeral. Our friends barbecued in our backyard. We wanted to be at home so the boys could be in and out with their friends but still close to us. We were sitting out in the backyard when a magnificent hawk swooped very low over our table with some delicious prey in its claws. It caught everyone's attention and as I looked up, I felt a chill go up and down me. I began to cry and Bruce put his arm around me. "I know that that's a sign from Ryan. He's telling me that he's okay. It's for my birthday." Bruce wondered why he didn't feel it also and I couldn't tell him why but I knew, as positively as I have ever known anything, that this was a sign from Ryan.

* * *

For Mother's Day, my girlfriend had an original watercolor painted for me of a hawk. It's called "Ryan's spirit" and is by a wonderful watercolor artist, Belinda Abendschein from Whispering Pines Designs in Waterford, Wisconsin. It reads:

I caught a glimpse of you, I'll forget it not, Just remember that for always, I'll love you will all my heart.

My friend's mom knew all about the hawk story and that she was giving me this watercolor. She was walking on the beach and casually talked to a man selling kites. He followed her as she was leaving and said he wanted to give her this one kite. *It was a hawk!* We decorated Ryan's grave for the first anniversary and the hawk was on his grave for the whole summer.

* * *

In February, my dad was continuing to have complications from open heart surgery and we were worried. Bruce and I had gone to the movies and then stopped afterwards to get something to eat. We ran into good friends of Ryan's. We started talking about Ryan's heatstroke and his friend told us the whole story as he had heard it from Josh and Matt, not knowing that there were some details that we'd never heard. He told us that when Ryan lost consciousness, he'd immediately had a seizure and lost control of his bladder and bowels. It just told me how very sick he must have felt and, as his mom, it hurt me so very much . I was very upset on the way home and then we found a phone message on our front table that my dad was back in the hospital again with pulmonary complications. Bruce just happened to check our e-mail to see if Dane had a baseball meeting the next day. He called me into the room because we had received an e-mail from Ryan's original address in Arizona. This account had been closed for a year... The subject entry said "I love you."

We didn't open it because we felt it was probably, logically, the "I love you" virus but I also felt it was a sign. I needed to hear that reassurance so very much from Ryan right then. I became convinced it was a sign when we did some investigating and learned that no one else on Ryan's address list received this e-mail other than Bruce's brother, Jim.

* * *

We also credit Ryan for beautiful skies and rainbows. Bruce and I were in Florida when Jake Frank's younger brother, Michael, died. We saw two connecting rainbows that night, one for Ryan and one for Mike. Brady wrote a beautiful paper on this in October.

* * *

We know that Ryan's spirit comes to us telling us to lighten up at times. On one particularly difficult day, there was a frog in my car that I know had come from the cemetery. On Mother's Day, I was very anxious. It seemed that every commercial on television carried a sentimental message and I was having such a tough time. We decided to take the boys to see *The Lion King* in Los Angeles as a special treat. We had dinner beforehand and, almost as soon as we were seated, Dane asked us what had just happened because he was covered in ketchup. We think the waiter tipped a tray that had a saucer of ketchup on it and that spilled on Dane but no one saw it happen. Bruce and Dane went to the bathroom to clean up. When we were eating dinner, Dane bent over to cut up his steak and we all started laughing because he had great globs of ketchup in his hair that Bruce couldn't see because Dane is so much taller! We think these little things come from Ryan to keep us laughing and to get us through some really tough moments.

Acknowledgment

Perhaps the most important lesson for the friends and family of the grieving is to learn how critical it is to acknowledge the pain. Someone has died, yes, but that person lives on in the hearts and memories of those who loved them. Remember. Acknowledge it. Say the name of the person who died. Talk about him. Be present with the pain of the grieving. **There is no reminding the grieving.** If someone grieving mentions their loved one ten times a day, please know that they have thought of their loved one five hundred times that day. In the Jewish faith, as long as a person is spoken about or thought about, he is remembered. Participate in remembering the one who has died.

Almost ten years ago, another family in our community lost two sons in a tragic car accident. I have always sent her a card on the anniversary of their passing. Before we lost Ryan, I had shared this with my sister, Candi, and she was concerned that my reminder might too painful. I knew, however, how much that family appreciated my cards. Candi now understands acknowledgment so very differently.

My sweet friend, Shelley, truly understood what it meant to be present with my pain. She sat with me again and again as I told the story of losing Ryan to different people. Each time she shed tears with me, I felt loved and supported.

Shelley is never afraid to bring something up to me that she thinks might be hard. Neither is my sister, Candi.

Bruce was at a meeting after another friend passed away, and the group was talking about a way to honor him. "Perhaps it's too soon; we wouldn't want to remind his widow." **There is no reminding the grieving.** She thinks about him all the time.

One friend was especially uncomfortable with my visible signs of grieving and thought she could help best by distracting me which didn't help at all. I happened to be sitting with her at a high school football game, three months after Ryan's death, and she introduced me to another parent sitting in front of us. Hearing my name, the mom asked me if I was Ryan Ferguson's mom. My eyes filled with tears as I answered, "Yes."

My friend jumped in, "She's also Graham and Brady and Dane's mom."

After the game, my friend apologized and said how badly that parent felt for making me cry. I hoped to make her understand. "I didn't cry because of anything she said. I cry because my son died and I'm sad. Sometimes my tears catch me off guard but please understand that I still cry everyday. My son died. I want people to remember him. The new fear is that no one will remember him. I am still his mom. She didn't make me cry."

The Funeral Franc always understood how important acknowledgment was to me. She always seemed to know how to reach out to me at a difficult time. I received a phone call from her on Christmas Eve. She's the head nurse in the Obstetrics unit and would be working all night. She told me that I could call her any time that night. She knew that we were dealing with the double whammy of Ryan's birthday and Christmas. Her acknowledgment felt so incredibly supportive.

When we would run into people in our community after Ryan's death, it was so uncomfortable if they didn't mention it. Did they not know that Ryan had died? The simple statements such as "We think of you everyday. We pray for you. We remember Ryan. I am so sorry." were all people needed to say and we appreciated their acknowledgment so very much. Most people did comment to us. For every one person who was clearly terrified that we might mention Ryan or cry or something, there were one hundred people who reached out to us. We were especially touched by the articulate ability of young people to acknowledge it. A Nordstrom shoe salesman asked me if I was Graham's mom because they'd gone to school together. He then told me how sorry he was that Ryan had died. Thank you, all of you young people especially, for possessing the poise and compassion to acknowledge our loss.

Bruce and I knew that there were some people on our Christmas card list who didn't know that Ryan had died and so we included a letter explaining what happened. What became impossible for us to understand were the people who didn't acknowledge that! How could we have been exchanging Christmas cards for all these years and when our child dies, nothing is said! We still struggle to understand that.

It helped us to have Ryan acknowledged in prayer, especially on holidays as we gathered together to say Grace before eating. This seems like such an appropriate time to mention Ryan, it felt hurtful to us when no one did.

Another dear friend was celebrating a special birthday and called to say, "I know this birthday party will be on the anniversary of Ryan's funeral and so that will be hard. We'd love to have you there, I hope you'll come." Her acknowledgment was so very considerate. We appreciated her thoughtfulness and went to the party.

Friends and family acknowledged the first anniversary. They called, sent flowers and cards, left things at Ryan's grave, and reached out to us again and again. People sent anniversary donations to Ryan's foundation. On a day which proved to be torturous for us, we were held and comforted by such acknowledgments. Thank you.

We decided it was important, not only to acknowledge again the generosity of our friends and family supporting Ryan's foundation, but also to acknowledge how we had used the donations.

The Ryan Ferguson Foundation

Dearest Friends and Family,

Thank you for your generous support of The Ryan Ferguson Foundation. We do appreciate your loving remembrance. Please know that we are continuously lifted by each one of you and we will never forget how you have reached out to our family since Ryan's passing.

The Ryan Ferguson Foundation has contributed to both the Y.M.C.A. campership program and the Villa Park High School Baseball Program in this first year. As you may know, Camp Bluff Lake was sold and the Orange Y.M.C.A. is in the process of purchasing a new camp with the generous help of Ron Clear. Club Wilderness in Running Springs is the site of camp for this year and may become the new Orange Y.M.C.A. camp. The Ryan Ferguson Foundation donated five camperships at Club Wilderness. Graham and Brady were both on staff for the first session of camp. There is a plaque at Camp Bluff Lake in Ryan's memory and once a new camp is purchased, Ryan will be honored there, as well. It reads:

Ryan Bruce Ferguson 1978-2000 Our friend, we will remember you, think of you, pray for you And when another day is through, we'll still be friends with you

The Villa Park High School Baseball Program held its first Easter Invitational Tournament this year and it was sponsored by The Ryan Ferguson Foundation. Villa Park played in the championship game. The high school team honored Ryan's memory by dedicating the season to him and wearing #28 on their sleeve. Since Dane was a part of this Varsity team, this was especially significant. The Booster Club also built a monument behind home plate remembering Ryan. It reads:

Ryan Bruce Ferguson #28 Varsity 1995-97 All League Pitcher May his love of sport live on through Spartan Baseball

Thank you again, The Fergusons

Comment of the Week

We had always been a joyous family. Bruce is very, very funny and his sense of humor has carried us through many, many stressful situations. We were not afraid to laugh. We were so heartbroken, so very sad most of the time, that we decided laughter was going to be guilt free. It was okay to laugh. And so, Bruce and I, privately at first, started the "Comment of the Week" contest. It carried us through the beginning.

It started in the first few days. Bruce had gone to the bank to withdraw all of the money we had set aside in a college fund for Ryan's senior year. We had to cover the costs of burying him. In the beginning, we both had a need to tell people what had happened and so Bruce told the teller who was helping him. She did offer appropriate sympathy but, when he left the bank, she cheerfully called out to him, "Maybe tomorrow will be a better day." We didn't think it would be better but it did give us the idea.

After that, we would each take the most bizarre thing said to us or weirdest reaction, and file it away as the "comment of the week."

Some of our favorite winners;

1. From the repairman who had made five unsuccessful trips to our house to fix our ice maker, "Your son died, and I'm having mortgage problems." Probably not the same.
2. From the hairdresser who cut my hair when my regular hairdresser was ill, "As a mother, all I would care about is that my child didn't have pain." Okay, but did you get the part that he died? I didn't want him to suffer, but we would have taken a little suffering if he had lived and been okay.

3. From a salesperson, "How annoying!"
1. From a parent whose son played on four soccer teams with Ryan, very jovially, "How's the family?" "We're doing okay; did you know that Ryan had passed away?" Even more jovial, "Yes, I heard that. How's the rest of the family?"
2. Hearing that I was writing this book, a friend's husband asked me, "Isn't it time you moved on?" Remember that there is no timetable to grief. It's a process. Do not say this to someone who is grieving.

A Calendar of Grieving

The First Month—July

G rief is overwhelming because it is so very painful. It can be frightening. Let yourself feel whatever comes. Talk about the one you have lost. Surround yourself with people who will listen. Try to make no final or new decisions right now about anything. Let a trusted friend help you with finances right now. Routine things you have always handled, like paying bills, can be overwhelming. Many people forget to make a house or car payment in the first few months. Set aside hospital bills for now in a folder. Let your friends and family help you through daily patterns. Remember, it is normal to feel numb. It is normal to feel anxious. It is normal to feel like this didn't really happen, like it's a dream, a nightmare, and you'll be waking up soon.

If you are taking medication prescribed by your doctor, be responsible. Sometimes there is a tendency to use alcohol or drugs more than usual. This response delays grief rather than resolving it. Try to sleep and to get some exercise. Pray. Remember to eat something. Journal.

* * *

My journal entry, July 9, 2000

I never knew hugs were so exhausting. We went to Dane's baseball game for Pony All Stars and saw so many people we hadn't yet seen. Their loving hugs drain me to the point of shaking.

Tonight I feel like screaming. I'm going back to work tomorrow and I don't know that I'm ready yet I know that I need to help my patients, and in doing so, I'll help myself.

My journal entry, July 11, 2000

Grief seems to come in waves like the ocean. The tide goes out and I can be peaceful and talk about Ryan's death calmly. Then I go to Target to buy picture frames and stuff for the boys to take to camp. The tide comes in and I find myself standing in a Target aisle with tears streaming down my face. It occurs to me that I'm buying frames for the last pictures I'll ever have of Ryan. I buy all the toiletries for camp in threes but it is so wrong because I always do this in "fours." Everything is so wrong and I find I can't pull myself out of the depths of this wave. I am drowning. A stranger stops and asks if I am okay.

My journal entry, July 12, 2000
I can still smell Ryan on his sheets but it's fading. How strange to be looking through your adult son's possessions. I'm not sure what I'm looking for....maybe something in his writing that would seem so poignant now. Mostly, I think I'm looking for Ryan.

Saturday morning, July 15, 2000

Today is my mom's real birthday. Was it really only three weeks ago that we were in Santa Barbara celebrating her seventy-fifth birthday with such joy? Today is a very different day. Today the boys left for camp. They have never gone without Ryan. We are driving up to camp tonight. There will be a memorial campfire for the counselors and our family after the regular campfire. It's too soon...too close to his funeral. How are we going to do this again? How are we going to make it through the week without the boys here?

Journal entry, July 19, 2000

I haven't written since the Memorial Campfire at Bluff Lake Saturday night. I was dreading it because it seemed to be so soon but what a tribute to Ryan. The 10:00 campfire was just for counselors, counselors-in-training, and us. Jeff Burgett started out, "Three younger brothers have lost their other..." and then he went on to talk about the fatherhood Ryan hadn't missed because for seven days a year, he was the very best dad—kind, loving, fair and gentle but he set boundaries. Perhaps the most moving tribute was from Nick Brooks, who held his hands to his head, as he told how he'd lost his best friend. Nick went on to say that he was in school because Ryan helped him to find college classes for kids with learning disabilities. I continue to be so very touched by Ryan's friends and what they say he meant to him. I have never been prouder of Ryan.

Graham and his friends left for Hawaii on their senior trip. Dane was going to play in the AAU National Baseball Tournament in Sarasota, Florida. We decided to go. Brady couldn't be convinced to join us. Bruce had to be in Boston for a couple of days first for business and it gave us a chance to see our dear friends. We would meet Dane in Florida.

Journal entry, July 27, 2000

Leaving the kids was brutal, just like when they were babies, and I hadn't anticipated that. I keep stumbling into situations that are hard—yet everything is hard. It's hard to go to a new gathering of people and see them for the first time. Tonight, I was dreading that first encounter with the PSNI group but it went okay. It was so good to see Ann and Jack especially. We sang and played guitar at Helene's house late. I really enjoyed it but then Helene's husband, Alan, sang a beautiful rendition of Eric Clapton's "Tears in Heaven" and once again, I couldn't stop the streaming of tears.

Journal entry, July 30, 2000

Flying from Boston to Florida early this morning, the young adult in the seat in front of me collapsed unconscious and fell on the passenger next to him. They summoned a doctor and carried him to the back of the plane where he was given oxygen and did, eventually, wake up. Seeing him so limp and unresponsive gave me a visual image of Ryan unconscious and how helpless he must have been. I just started sobbing.

Checking cell phone messages, we learned that Dane's classmate, Mike Frank, age 14, had passed away after a long battle with a brain tumor. A mutual friend, not knowing we're in Florida, and not knowing how we are, asked if I would call Mike's parents to offer some first hand insight. I would never share with a more newly bereaved parent how we are at this time. When people ask, we usually say that we're hanging in there or we're doing okay or maybe we talk about the tides of grief. But how would it help to know that since the first few days of agonizing horror, it has gotten no better? Bruce and I both cry everyday. Often we fall asleep sobbing in each other's arms. The first thing we think of each morning is that Ryan is dead and we think of that all day long. Every experience is tainted because Ryan will never experience it. The depths of the pain and the sadness we feel are indescribable and how would it help the Franks to know the rawness that lies ahead? I hope that they can find some comfort that Mike's suffering has ended just as we take some comfort that Ryan didn't suffer. But, that doesn't help with the daily agony that is with us every waking hour right now.

I did send the Franks a letter from Florida. Brady is close friends with Mike's older brother, Jake, and he was a pall-bearer at Mike's funeral. My sister was there with Brady and, thank God, for the easy communication of cell phones.

We encouraged Brady by reminding him just how much everyone's support meant to us but it seemed so soon to have him face something like this. Brady is an incredibly com-passionate teenager and he had the strength to do what most people cannot. We are so very proud of him.

We all find it very comforting to have something of Ryan's with us. I carry his copy of "Footprints" in my wal-let. Bruce took Ryan's brand new glasses and had his pre-scription put in the frames. He loves wearing them. One of the funniest times was when Bruce was wearing what he thought was Ryan's t-shirt. Ryan was very thin and so this t-shirt was a bit snug on Bruce and he kept pulling on it all day. Graham asked him that night, "Dad, why are you wearing my shirt?" It turned out that Ryan had "borrowed" this shirt from Graham quite a while ago and Graham had been looking for it.

The Second Month — August

There are common physical characteristics of grief. Some people experience a tightness in the throat or heaviness in the chest. It is normal to lose your appetite or to feel like eating all the time. Chronic tiredness is another common characteristic. Many people feel dizzy, headachy and short of breath. These symptoms could also be indicative of a serious health concern. Grief also stresses your auto-immune system. Make an appointment with your physician for a check-up. Don't count on your usual abilities to assess your own health. The physical symptoms of grief mimic real health problems. We all had check-ups right away.

When your insurance company has paid their portion of the medical bills, you need to address your co-payments. Many hospitals will negotiate your portion of the bills, accept insurance payments as payment in full or will be willing to set up a payment plan for you. Most ambulance companies are not providers for insurance companies and set their own rates. This means that your insurance company will pay their portion and the ambulance company will expect full payment on the remainder of the balance from you. Check **into this. It is sometimes possible to negotiate.**

* * *

I was under a doctor's care for hyperthyroidism and Graves' disease when Ryan died but Bruce hadn't had a physical in a while. I felt we needed to reassure the boys that we were okay, since the unthinkable had already happened, and so, with my firm encouragement, Bruce had had a physical before we left for Florida. We got the phone message while we were there that Bruce had Type II Diabetes! This was completely unexpected since Bruce had absolutely no symptoms, but we try to look at it as a blessing of Ryan's death. Bruce has a chance to control it with diet, exercise and medication and, hopefully, avoid the serious complications of undetected diabetes. Bruce, a dessert lover, did complain some, "First my son dies; now I'm supposed to give up chocolate!"

We didn't want people to feel guarded around us, as if there were things that couldn't be said like using the word "brain dead." However, we all flinched when one mom on the baseball team kept saying, "They're all going to have a heatstroke, and it's so hot!"

Journal entry August 5, 2000

Home to California today. Dane's team finished tenth, not the first they had hoped for. They were 6—0 going into a Sudden Death Championship round. They lost 4—2. It occurs to me how much life is like baseball. The best guys don't always win, things aren't always fair, prayers aren't always answered with the answer you want but you give it your best to win. The only way not to lose is not to play, not to love.

We saw Ryan's buddy, Matt Boone, play at Lakeland last night. He is so handsome and so full of life and promise, so much like Ryan that my chest hurt as we hugged goodbye and said "We love you."

I ordered Ryan's headstone. I finally decided that I liked the ones with the picture on it. It's unbelievable how expensive a headstone is! I wanted to use the word "cherished" instead of "beloved," it just sounds younger.

Cherished son and brother Grandson, nephew, cousin, friend Ryan Bruce Ferguson December 25, 1978—June 25, 2000 Spirit, mind, body

An 8' by 10" picture of Ryan would be on the left side of it. Under the picture I added, "Forever in our hearts." The "Spirit, Mind Body" is the YMCA triangle. It would take six to eight weeks for the headstone to be finished.

A friend from early married days came with me to buy flowers for Ryan's grave. It was my first time putting anything in his vases and I appreciated her company so very much. She brought me a copy of a poem which had helped her when her mother passed away. I came to love it!

Don't cry at my grave Cause I won't be there I'll be in the breeze That ruffles your hair

I'll be in the sunshine I'll be in the snow I'll be in the places Where we used to go

I'll be in your laughter And in funny things I'll be in your shadow And there in your dreams

I'll be in your greetings But not your good-byes I'll be in the reflection Of your loving eyes I'll always be with you And I'll always care So don't cry at my graveside Cause I won't be there

Author Unknown

Saturday, August 26, 2000

The coroner's office called at home with the long awaited autopsy results. Ryan had been dead for two months and now we would know why. He died of complications of a heatstroke, nothing more. The toxicology report detected nothing other than small traces of caffeine, no drugs or alcohol. His lungs showed small traces of the virus Ryan had had two weeks before he died, nothing particularly significant, but he was listing it as a possible contributing factor to the heatstroke. "It's as if he was struck by lightning," the coroner said. "I can't really tell you why a healthy twenty-one-year old male would fall victim to a heatstroke under these conditions." The coroner went on to explain the fatal complications of the heatstroke, including D.I.C. (disseminating intravascular coagulation). We knew at the hospital that Ryan had lost his ability to coagulate his blood. This is a fatal complication of heatstroke. He agreed to send me a copy of the autopsy report.

Bruce and I sat down with the boys and explained why their brother had died. Graham expressed a lot of relief because he, as he now told us, had been worried that there was something genetically wrong and that they all had it. He confessed he'd had stomach pains since Ryan's passing. We were able to reassure the boys and then Bruce and I fled to the cemetery. Somehow, this felt like another blow. I guess I had hoped it would turn out to be a brain aneurysm, something that would have been impossible to detect or prevent. A heatstroke just still seemed unbelievable, water would have made a difference, and yet they were drinking water and Gatorade that day.

People that don't know us well don't understand how safety conscious we have always been. We taught the boys to wear seat-belts and helmets. When we were at the river, they wore sunscreen, life jackets and drank lots of fluids. It felt somehow ironic to me that Ryan had died of a heat-stroke. I understood, from the very beginning, that others needed his death to be attributed to something different. If Ryan had died doing something risky, then others could just tell their children not to do that and they'd be safe. One of the reasons Ryan's death touched our community in such an overwhelming way is that no one could feel safe. If Ryan died from a heatstroke, then someone else could too. There was no way to distance themselves from our tragedy.

One friend told me that another parent had asked her what the "real story" was, what really caused Ryan's death. Even though this friend understood from the beginning that there were only two possibilities, a heat stroke or an aneurysm, she backed away from what she thought would be a potential confrontation by saying that she didn't know.

I felt somewhat letdown. It was obvious to me that the "real story" would have to come from us.

The Third Month—September

You need time during grief; time alone and time with others who will listen when you want to talk and who will be with you when you need to cry. Remember to eat, exercise and rest. Allow yourself to take "mini-breaks" from your grief. It's okay to be diverted. Don't be afraid to have fun. Laughter helps.

It is normal to worry that you might be losing your mind or to yearn for life as it used to be. Feeling forgetful or disoriented, experiencing a lack of energy and a sense of vulnerability are all normal parts of the grief process. Many people feel depressed, as if life now has no meaning. It can feel isolating to be so sad when others around you appear to have happy lives. Many people replay memories of the last few days, weeks or hours. This is normal. Some people dream vividly about the one who has died or don't dream at all. You may experience sudden changes of mood. Moods will pass. Feeling angry at God or angry at the person who died is common. Know that time will help. Give yourself time. Be as patient with yourself as you would be with someone else who was grieving.

* * *

The boys are back in school. Dane has started high school and Brady is a junior. One of Graham's first decisions after Ryan died was that he would not move into an apartment his first year of college. He would be playing baseball at Irvine Valley Community College and we were so grateful he chose to stay home. We needed him to be at home.

I drive by the cemetery on my way to work so I honk twice as I go by. Bruce drives that way often, also, and he honks. It makes us feel like we're saying "hi."

I gave Crosby's fiancée a shower. It was something I had planned to do before Ryan's passing. It seemed like it was important to still do this. We were flying to Lake Tahoe as a family for their wedding on September 29th. I felt like I was propelling myself forward but dragging a heavy anchor.

People tell us that we were a "role model" for family life and now we're a "role model" for how to say good-bye. I don't want to be. I just want Ryan back. Another woman, who had lost a child, told Bruce, "You will spend a lifetime trying to make this be okay. It will never be okay." We understood what she meant exactly.

The Fourth Month—October

Firsts are always painful for someone grieving; the first family celebration, first holidays, first birthdays without your loved one. Anticipating that it may be difficult may help you to be prepared with some coping strategies. It is normal to feel that nothing is normal.

In the fourth month, you begin a new "quarter" of grieving. You are beyond the initial paralyzing shock and now are left to begin to deal with the loss. This is the time to connect with support outside of your circle of friends if you have not already done so. There are support groups for every kind of loss. You may find both comfort and hope from those who have experienced a similar loss. Knowing some things that helped them, and realizing that they have recovered may give you hope that your grief will not always feel this raw and painful. You can connect to support groups through churches, friends and the internet. A friend sent us our first newsletter of "The Compassionate Friends" and I found it very helpful. Bruce, however, hated reading it. It is normal to have different reactions to the same thing. The social worker at the hospital where your **loved one died can also be a resource for support groups. If your loved one was receiving hospice care, they will provide support for the grieving family.**

Consider grief counseling. A therapist can provide a safe place to explore the grieving process. Some people begin counseling immediately. In cases of suicide or violent death, this is often the best choice. Other people find that they are in so much shock during the first three months, that they weren't ready to begin counseling until later. In individual counseling, you may be able to express common feelings of anger, resentment, bitterness and frustration that you hold back in front of family and friends for fear of worrying or hurting them. Therapy will normalize your feelings and give you new coping strategies. The therapist will provide a structure to this first year of grieving and help you to know what to expect. Individual and family grief counseling will be very helpful to guide you through this journey.

* * *

October 1st, 2000, journal entry

Today was Crosby and Kristin's wedding…at 8:00 A.M.! I had been fine through all the pre-wedding festivities. Bruce and I had had a very nice time yesterday with my nephew, Travis, his bride, Sharie and her family. Candi and Taylor hosted a wonderful Rehearsal Dinner. Everything went very well. The wedding itself was so difficult.

We were seated in the hall for the wedding and there were six seats in each row. For some reason, they kept moving us and each time we had to change rows, I kept counting the seats and there were only five of us now so I started crying. This was what Ryan would never have, and we would never get to share with him….a wedding. Ryan and Natalie had been dating about the same amount of time that Crosby and Kristin had… it was a gut-wrenching ceremony for me. I

tried to cry silently so that my sadness wouldn't ruin any-
thing for anyone else.

Tuesday, October 10th

I felt drawn to the cemetery today but I didn't know why.
I stopped to see Ryan and thought perhaps I was at the wrong
grave, but that wasn't what was different. I turned around
and there was Ryan staring back at me from his headstone.
It is so beautiful but somehow, so very painfully final, to see
this. I called Bruce so that he could see it before he left for
his five day men's horseback ride. Matt called me that night.
"Pam, when did the headstone go in?" Matt had had a dream
about Ryan and in his dream; Matt saw them installing the
headstone. He'd gone to the cemetery on Tuesday morning
and it was already in.

I thought we were ready as a family to begin grief
counseling. The boys thought that I could do this for them
but I knew that I could not. I was a grieving mother and
needed someone else's guidance to help us through this first
year. A dear colleague, Dr. Kim Storm, was a perfect choice.
His style was similar to mine and so the boys would find
it familiar, but he was a man and that would feel different.
Bruce and I wanted to do this for the boys. We wanted them
to have every chance to heal and not have their lives be forever marked by their brother's death. Thursday, October 19th
was our first appointment. We began to talk, as a family,
about this loss. With Kim's guidance, over the course of
the next nine months, we began the journey of healing. We
never came away from a counseling session without some
new understanding of how the boys felt, and they would
say the same thing about us. It was gut-wrenchingly painful
at times, but also healing, and so very important to us all.
Thank you, Kim.

Thursday, October 26, 2000

Our Christmas card picture has always been a special project. I take great pride in our cards. There is always a picture; a professional one since we have had Dane. Bruce and I are in the picture in even-numbered years. Each year I write the verse. There is always a theme. There have been years when the project became overwhelming with some idea that included hand-coloring or bow tying. My cards are a little bit famous. The boys joke that once you get on the list, you're always on the list and it must now include most of Orange County (it doesn't). One of the things that I discussed with my girlfriends, in the first few horrific days after Ryan's death, was my Christmas cards. How would I do one now? We always took the picture in October and it was time.

As our new family of five drove to take the picture, Ryan's spirit was with us. Graham (sorry, Buddy) had a horrible stomach ache that was threatening to erupt at any moment and so we told our dear friend and photographer, Michael Good, that we had to take the picture quickly before Graham threw up. This distracted us, for a moment, from what we were doing, and we quickly got several shots of one pose. Michael asked us if we wanted to try a different pose, but the gravity of the moment caught up with me and I burst into tears. "That will be the pose!" Bruce said. We got out of there and Graham soon felt better.

The Fifth Month — November

It is normal to feel that you have "unfinished business" with the person who died. It may be helpful to write a letter about what you wish you had said, or done, or hadn't said or done. Pour out your feelings. Tell them goodbye. You may want to leave this letter at the grave. You may need to write several times.

You need at least one person with whom you can share your grief. A physical release for anger such as running or kick-boxing can be very helpful. Find a special place where you can let out your feelings or be alone with your grief.

* * *

We got the proofs back from Michael and, as a family, decided on our dedication to Ryan. Ryan was, as all the boys are, a huge Dave Matthews fan. There is a line from one of his songs, "Life is short but sweet for certain." The boys had wanted it on Ryan's headstone but Bruce and I felt it would be dated soon so, in a family compromise, we agreed it would be on the Christmas card.

In loving memory of Ryan! Happy Birthday! December 25, 1978—June 25, 2000 "Life is short but sweet for certain." Dave Matthews

Family, faith and friends are the greatest blessings!

Merry Christmas from the Fergusons Bruce, Pam, Graham, Brady and Dane

Dane had a difficult time understanding why Ryan's name wasn't listed with the rest of ours since he's still a part of our family. I'm with Dane on this one. I still have a difficult time writing our family names and excluding Ryan.

* * *

Bruce and I flew to New Orleans for a business meeting. Our dear friends from Atlanta met us there. We've been good, good friends for years. She supports me with prayer and scripture via e-mail. I am blessed to have this friendship.

* * *

We always have had Thanksgiving with my dad and his wife, Arlene. For the past several years, we'd had Thanksgiving at their Lake Arrowhead home so we decided to continue that this year. I had such a feeling of Ryan's presence in their cabin. I could see him wrestling with his brothers or talking to my dad last year. I missed him so deeply. That night, sleeping in my dad's Lake Arrowhead cabin, I had the first of what would become a recurring nightmare. I dreamt that Ryan was standing in the doorway but I couldn't get to him. I awakened Bruce, and others, with my screams. This was the first dream I had had about Ryan. I was always aware that Ryan was dead when I was sleeping and I had decided, that somehow, I was controlling my dreams so that unchecked hospital images would not come back to me all night long. How I wish I could dream about him as he lived, so joyfully! I wanted those dreams!

Over Thanksgiving weekend, Dane played in a baseball tournament. He had pitched particularly well in one game and I talked to him that night. It was November 25th.

"Mom, do you know what today is?" referring to the five-month anniversary.

"Yes, Daner, I was remembering that also. Dane, you pitched really well today." Normally, I would stop there since Dane is a man of few words, but this time I decided to continue. "Dane, I believe that when you do something really, really well, or when something great happens to you, that Ryan sees it in heaven and he is cheering for you also. He saw you today and he's so proud of you."

Long, long pause and then he answered, "Mom, I pray to Ryan before I pitch. When you see me take a knee, I am praying to Ryan and to God. And when you see me bend over to stretch, I am stretching, but I am also praying to Ryan and God." This was the day I knew that Dane would be okay, that he had found a way to make this make sense for him and I cherish that conversation.

The Sixth Month — December

I often advise my patients to pick a day, usually the birthday of the loved one, to remember that person each year, to celebrate the life. It is important to establish new rituals for your family around the holidays and special occasions. Give yourself permission to do what feels "right" the first year, even if you change the new ritual after that. It is okay to eat pizza instead of preparing a special feast this first year. It is okay not to do all the things you usually do.

Many grieving people find that the sixth month is often a low point in the first year of grieving. Should the sixth month coincide with a holiday, ours was the triple blow of the first Christmas, Ryan's real birthday and this sixth month time, it can be especially difficult. Friends and family have returned to their lives but your loved one is still gone. Let people know how you are honestly. Let people know what you might need. Most people don't know how to support someone in grief. It is not their fault that they don't know what to say or do. Continue to love your family and friends. Find small ways to show it. Love your family and yourself.

* * *

We decided that, for this year at least, we would hang Ryan's stocking and put his "gingerbread man" by the front door. As emotional as we were decorating the house for Christmas, it seemed like it would feel worse to exclude him. Bruce and I knew that some people on our Christmas list didn't know that Ryan had passed away and so I wrote a letter and included it with those cards.

Dearest Friends,

As you may already know, Ryan died suddenly after suffering a cerebral hemorrhage caused by a heatstroke. He had been dirt bike riding outside of Banning for less than two hours when he fell unconscious. He was taken first to San Gorgonio Hospital and later transported to Loma Linda where he died. He never regained consciousness but lived long enough for the five of us, grandparents, aunts, uncles, cousins and friends to get to the hospital and surround him in love and prayer as he died. Final autopsy results confirmed that he died from complications of a heatstroke—no head injury, drugs or alcohol. Ryan died on June 25th, the day we always celebrated his Christmas birthday. We are absolutely heartbroken but continue to be lifted up by the tremendous outpouring of love and support shown to us during this most difficult time of our lives.

Ryan was a student at the University of Arizona in Tucson, majoring in Communications. He planned to graduate in 2001 and loved his summer internship in commercial real estate. People were drawn to Ryan by his ready smile, they stayed to enjoy his sense of humor and share his zest for life, earning him a richness in friends beyond his years. More than anything, Ryan loved being the big brother and friend. His passions were Snowboarding, being at "The River" counseling at the YMCA Camp Bluff Lake and playing baseball.

The Ryan Ferguson Foundation has been established in his honor to support camperships to Camp Bluff Lake and the Villa Park High School Baseball Program. To find out more about his foundation or to see his eight-minute memorial video, check out *www.ryanfergusonfoundation.com*

We know that Ryan continue to touch the lives of so many people. Please cherish your relationships. We truly believe that family, faith and friends are the greatest blessings! God bless you and Merry Christmas!

The Fergusons

Brady's birthday is December 7th. It was also a counseling day. It seemed sadly ironic and yet somehow appropriate that our birthday celebration would follow therapy. I find it impossible to get through "Happy Birthday" without crying but the day will come when I can do that.

We attended Christmas Eve services at Trinity Presbyterian where we had had Ryan's funeral. I found it impossible to sing Christmas carols and I love to sing. The new goal was to cry quietly. Nick Brooks came over after church and told me how many of Ryan's friends had found Christ since his passing. I am grateful for that but I still wish that I had Ryan and they had become Christians a different way.

My mom and Art came for Christmas Eve and Day as they always do. Mom was sick with a bronchial virus and we were emotional. Not a lot of fun! Mom and Art went to bed early. Bruce and I were toasting Ryan's birthday at midnight when Graham burst into the family room. He was in Ryan's room and found a practically full bottle of *Joop* cologne and he considered it a gift from Ryan! He came to show us and the five of us huddled together and sang Happy Birthday to Ryan! We all went to bed then except for Bruce. I awakened an hour or so later and went downstairs. I found Bruce crying, trying to write me a Christmas card, to tell me how much he loved me, but the pain of this Christmas without Ryan was too great and the words wouldn't come.

"Come to bed, sweetheart. I know you love me."

And so it was Christmas Day. Ryan's twenty-second birthday. The Santa Ana winds had howled all night, which made everything especially miserable. We opened presents. I surprised everyone with a picture of Ryan. Michael, the photographer, had gone back through old Christmas pictures, and we had both really liked this one picture of Ryan taken with his brothers in 1997. He had isolated Ryan's face and made copies of it for everyone. I gave them as Christmas presents in beautiful silver frames from Ryan. Graham teased that Ryan had really shopped early.

After breakfast, we went as a family to the cemetery. The winds were still howling and everything was blowing. All the beautiful Christmas decorations left on graves were blown all over. We held hands as a family and tried to find some of Ryan's things. We did find his packet of letters and most of his decorations. The boys remarked on this special Christmas tradition....walking the cemetery looking for your brother's things!

My sister came for dinner with her family. We have always had a tradition of Ryan having a Christmas tree shaped cake on his birthday, even though we celebrated his birthday on his half-birthday. Candi baked the tree cake for Ryan and our doorbell started to ring. Ryan's friends, this close-knit, wonderful group of young adults, dropped in on us all afternoon and evening. We sang together, family and friends, and wished Ryan a Happy Birthday.

The Seventh Month—January

Initially, when a tragedy occurs, family and friends set aside difficulties and unite in support of those grieving the hardest. However, people don't usually change in core ways unless they really work to change and so relationships return to the dynamics that preceded the death. This can be very disheartening because the journey of grieving is overwhelming in itself, without adding anything else, but this "return" is normal for people and relationships.

* * *

January 1, 2001 journal entry

Don't tell me you know Christmas was difficult and then say it was hard for you, too. Ask me and listen. I talked to both Nan and Jeanne (Bruce's sister and mother) tonight. I thanked Nan for going by the cemetery when we were gone in Mammoth skiing and she told me how hard it was to find and how her kids (ages 18 and 20) didn't want to go but they were glad they did. Then she told me that her mom said Ryan was a ghost. Jeanne tells me she thinks of us daily but neither of them really asks. I think they are afraid to know....

Do you want to know what it's really like? That I couldn't stop the tears from streaming down my face on Christmas Eve during church? The new goal became not to make noise. Do you want to know how I found your son and brother sobbing, all alone on Christmas Eve? When you tell me you know our Christmas was hard, do you want to know this? Do you really want to know what this is like for your son and brother? What do you think it's like for Graham, Brady and Dane to go to the cemetery? I wish you would both be brave enough to ask.

I recognize my anger in this journal entry. I understood that I wanted more from Jeanne and Nan than they could probably give. I knew how much they were hurting and that it was difficult for them to express it to us. It didn't help us to avoid the subject but there was no malice intended. I believe they both felt helpless.

Our parents were all really struggling with how to help us. They had watched their grandson die and now they were watching their children grieve deeply. Grandparents are often considered the "forgotten mourners" but their pain is very real and doubly edged. I understood this all too well because as overwhelming as the pain was to have lost Ryan, it hurt me even more to see the raw grief of Graham, Brady and Dane.

It took me a long time to recognize that, on some level, I was angry with people who were trying to avoid our pain. I understood that it was uncomfortable for them, but, since I was struggling at times just to have the strength to breathe, didn't they also have to reach deeply inside themselves to face what was uncomfortable for them? No, people didn't. I needed to accept that I was angry about this and then I could better accept others for where they were in dealing with death. I think I had mistakenly concluded that since I wasn't angry with God for taking Ryan or at Ryan for dying, that I wouldn't be angry. It is okay and normal to be angry.

The after Christmas letdown is really getting to Bruce. I see how depressed he is and so Tim and Shelley planned a little surprise party for his January 11th birthday. This small gathering of friends truly lifted Bruce's spirits and, when he is okay, I am okay. Tim and Shelley continually amaze us with their ability to be there and our friendship began with Ryan and their son, Chris.

Letter from the Flathers when Ryan died

I'll never forget the first time I met you Ryan—a smiling kindergarten boy of five curly hair, freckled face and very knobby knees. Chris said, "This is my friend Ryan Ferguson, can he come to our house to play?"

Ryan, as smart as he could be, said, "My number is 9986— and I can come today!"

So the journey of the Ferguson-Flathers friendship began—thanks to the very first meeting of Ryan Ferguson, the kindergarten boy with his sweet freckled face grin.

The boys have always been great about making curfews and we really work to not be overprotective. We have tried to let the boys continue to do all the things they did before Ryan died. However, Brady fell asleep at a friend's house and was late coming home. I've never been an anxious mom. I always believed that "Bad news would find you" and this was certainly the case when Ryan died. But when Brady was late, all I could think of was that we were going to have to face another tragedy and so that twenty minutes of waiting for him was totally tortuous for me!

Wednesday, January 24, 2001

My dad had open heart surgery to replace a heart valve. I keep telling my dad that Ryan doesn't need him. Ryan is fine. I need him! Bruce, Candi and I drove to Palm Desert to wait with Arlene while he has the surgery. It was raining and it took us a while to get there. He was already out of surgery and he was fine! We went into see him and the image of my dad with all these tubes brought me right back to hospital images of Ryan. The tears streamed down my face again.

Brady went Snowboarding with his good friend, Adam. Adam missed the jump and, by the time Brady got to him, he was unconscious and his head was bleeding. Adam went to the hospital and Brady knew he'd be okay when he called me. I'd love to protect my boys from anything which re-triggers horrific images of their brother dying but that doesn't seem possible. I could hardly wait until Brady arrived home so I could hug him!

The Eighth Month—February

I t will be helpful to find a project or a cause which you can devote time and energy to that will carry a personal attachment to your lost loved one. It will give you a focus and again validate the life lost.

* * *

Dane's birthday is February 14th and he is sick again. We went out together as a family to celebrate but he ended up throwing up in the parking lot. Dane continues to have night sweats and throws up frequently now. I think this is another grief reaction rooted in anxiety.

* * *

My dad has had a series of complications and re-hospitalizations since his surgery. I am not ready to lose him. I believe that God slowly revealed to me the whole story of Ryan's death as I would be ready to understand it. I don't believe that the young adult who collapsed on the airplane in the seat in front of us, or running into Ryan's friends and hearing about that day was a coincidence. I needed time to begin to understand all that had happened.

* * *

Travis and Sharie are moving to Boston. This is Candi's oldest son and, of course, she is grieving the loss. I understand that "I win" the Loss Contest most of the time but there is real loss everywhere. I don't want Candi, or anyone, to think that they can't talk to me about their hurt because my hurt is greater. I don't want anyone to feel that way. I need to be a friend and a sister, too. Please let me.

The Ninth Month—March

There is no way to hurry the journey of healing. It is normal to feel that you are making great progress in accepting the loss and then to have several blue days in a row. Forgive yourself over and over again, for the past, for your feelings, for anything real or imaginary. Write again to your loved one if you have more unfinished business. Do not let others rush you in your grieving. If you rush yourself, you will delay your healing.

* * *

A friend of mine was diagnosed with cancer and the initial prognosis is not optimistic. Her son is close friends with Dane and had been one of the people who supported Dane when Ryan died. Dane pulled me aside and told me about his conversation with his friend. His buddy had asked Dane why these things happen. "My mom says the *whys* will make you crazy." Even if Dane doesn't always participate in conversations, I know he's listening. I am grateful for that.

I do believe the *whys* will make you crazy. I never let myself think "Why my son and not someone else's son?

Why not that murderer's son or that kid who is drug-addicted?" I never let myself go there. I wouldn't wish this on the worst person in the world. I think the true question is not "Why me?" but, rather, "Why not me?" Why would I ever think that I should be spared tragedy?

Graham is having a tough time. He never wanted to be the oldest brother and now that is his role. Graham has always loved baseball, has always had such "heart" when he plays. Now he doesn't. He has taken the year off. He doesn't like his community college.. He has applied to Arizona State University for the fall term. He understands that he's throwing everything in the same emotional pot. We are spending a lot of time together talking.

I go to the cemetery every week. On Thursdays, I make a quick stop on my way to work to pick up Ryan's things so he won't lose them when they mow. Late on Fridays, I bring fresh flowers to Ryan and put his things back. Sometimes I sit and read the letters and notes his friends have left in the freezer bag mailbox. I take care of his grave because it makes me feel like I am still his mom. I read that very description in one of the "Compassionate Friends" newsletters and found it very reassuring that other moms felt this same way.

The Tenth Month—April

The stages of grief are denial, anger, bargaining, depression and acceptance. However, not everyone experiences each stage and your path may jump from emotion to emotion. It is normal to feel like you're on a roller coaster. It is normal to plan for big events like holidays and then be unprepared for an intense emotional reaction to some small trigger. It is sometimes the trivial things which create the most perplexing emotions. Be patient with these reactions. Be patient with yourself.

* * *

The Villa Park High School Baseball Team is dedicating the season to Ryan. The foundation is sponsoring the Easter tournament and so the team will wear their #28 patches for the first time and dedicate the monument on the opening day of the tournament. Instead it rained, poured actually. It was postponed to Monday, April 9th, before the first game. This happened to be Graham's birthday. The dedication was very bittersweet. We were deeply touched by this honor but it was still very raw. We made fliers for the snack bar explaining what had happened and sharing a special baseball moment:

Remember Ryan #28

"Ryan was an All League First Team, left-handed pitcher for Villa Park High School, on Varsity from 1995-97. One of his favorite baseball memories was getting the win against Canyon on April 24th, 1997, in a game televised on Fox West Sports Two as the high school game of the week."

The Ryan Ferguson Foundation is proud to sponsor the Villa Park Easter Invitational Baseball Tournament. As a family, we are so very touched by the memorial plaque and that the Spartan Baseball Team is wearing #28 this season. Thank you for honoring Ryan in such a special way. We will always cherish the outpouring of love and support we have received since his passing.

Bruce, Pam, Graham, Brady and Dane Ferguson

* * *

I continue to have unexpected "grief attacks." I was referred to an endocrinologist who specializes in hyperthyroidism and Graves' disease. I waited a month before I could get in for an appointment. Filling out paperwork, I came to a page where it asked me to list family members; parents, siblings, children... living and deceased. I started sobbing in his office waiting room and had to go outside to collect myself. I continue to be surprised by these attacks. The only good thing I could say about this one is that the nurse, put me in a waiting room ahead of other people because I was so upset!

The Eleventh Month—May

There is no one "right" time to do things along your journey. It is often extremely painful to go through the things of the loved one but it can be very cathartic for those grieving. People often regret giving personal items away too quickly and family members often complain about the bedroom or house being turned into a "shrine." Agree as a family on a time when you're ready to go through things and decide what to keep and give away. Find a balance between "too soon" and the "shrine" extremes. We went through some of Ryan's things when they came home from the University of Arizona, and agreed to go through the rest before Graham left for college. Do not do this task alone.

* * *

Bruce read a story in the paper about another local boy, aged 21, who was killed in a car accident. I contacted the paper and reached his mom. It turned out that she was good friends with another friend of mine. We all had breakfast together. Her son, Justin, is buried near Ryan. Sometimes, I see her at the cemetery and we talk together. I feel I am in a position to offer strength now. I am in such a different place than I was when Michael Frank died. I was too raw to help anyone, then. I feel compelled to reach out to Barbara. Her son, Justin, was her only child and my heart just breaks for her. I never felt invalidated when people would tell me "at least you have other children." I always felt very blessed to have the boys. It is impossible for me to comprehend the pain of losing your only child.

* * *

It's graduation time and I find the announcements bitter-sweet. Ryan should have been graduating now. My mom is going to be on a trip over Mother's Day. I was anxious about this celebration so we decided to go to see *The Lion King* as a family and it was such a perfect change. We had a wonderful time.

Bruce wrote me a card inspired from The Lion King:

He's a part of you
He's a part of me
He lives on in each of us

The boys seem to be thriving. They truly haven't skipped a beat. We haven't seen grades or attitudes plummet. Dane was Student of the Month for his Freshman Honors History class. Graham was accepted at Arizona State University as a sophomore and we're busy organizing housing for him. He leaves in August.

Brady was the one I worried about the most when Ryan died. In many ways, he was the closest to Ryan. It had always been Ryan and Brady, Graham and Dane. This is how they had paired up in terms of temperament, interests and personalities. Brady is the one most like Ryan and I had worried he'd be lost without his bookend. However, Brady has this incredible ability to express himself and to be joyful. Therefore, Bruce and I watched, with great pride, as an "Abe Lincoln-like" Brady gave a take off on the Gettysburg address in a school assembly when he ran for an ASB office. Brady was elected as the Commissioner of Recognition for his Senior Year, a job which requires him to plan and host all the Student of the Month Luncheons. He'll be awesome.

* * *

Brady and Graham are both going with friends to the Dave Matthews' concerts. Music has always triggered so many memories. Dave Matthews was a favorite of Ryan's and it was impossible for either boy to be at his concert without fresh waves of grief.

The Twelfth Month—June

F ew grieving families are prepared for the impact of the first anniversary. It is normal to relive the loss and the pain of the death but do not let the pain blind you from your joyful memories. It is the gift of the life and the cherished memories that will carry you forward. It is the final "first."

The Anniversary

E-mail to friends June 22, 2001

Hi Guys!

*It's impossible to believe that Ryan has been gone for a year but the first anniversary will be Monday. Dane left for Tucson last night to play baseball in the Junior Olympic Tournament and Graham and Brady leave in the morning for camp. Bruce and I are leaving Sunday morning for Tucson to join Dane. Graham is going to have Ryan's brown rag tied on him Monday night in the Ragger's ceremony. He has planned this for a year. We are all finding special ways to remember and to move forward. We continue to be over-*whelmed by the loving support of friends like you. Thank you for being there for us this year.

Graham is convinced that I talk myself into being anxious so I really tried not to build up the first anniversary of Ryan's death to be something huge. We had made it a year. We could make it through this. Camp Bluff Lake had been sold and the boys would be at a new temporary location, Club Wilderness, this year. The first session of camp would be during the week of the anniversary. Graham and Brady would be there as counselors. Dane was going to be in Tucson, Arizona, playing baseball in the Junior Olympics Championship Tournament. Bruce and I would join him on Sunday, June 24th in Tucson. Tim and Shelley were celebrating their twenty-fifth wedding anniversary on June 23rd and I was singing at the party. This was our plan. We had made it a year.

We'd be fine. I put an announcement in the paper remembering Ryan and mailed in a birthday tribute to *The Compassionate Friends* newsletter.

Sunday, June 24th, 2001

Bruce and I were flying Southwest to Tucson and we were in separate boarding groups. I overheard some parents talking and realized they were going to the University of Arizona Parents' Weekend. Ryan had attended the University of Arizona. We were one of those parents just a short time ago. I sat down next to Bruce and recognized the shirt he was wearing as the shirt he'd worn when Ryan died. This began our two-day, torturous ordeal of the anniversary. We were obsessed with the timeline. Now this is what was happening. This is what the doctor said.

This is how Ryan looked. We had both spent time alone with Ryan in Tucson and it seemed that everywhere we went, we had memories. It felt as if we were saying goodbye to him all over again. Dane had a game in the morning of June 25th and I caught his eye in the dug-out when it was 11:22 A.M.

We kept calling home and hearing messages from friends and family. It meant so very much to us both. My friend, Nancy, called me just at dusk to let me know what Ryan's grave looked like now. There were notes and flowers everywhere. This lifted us up so very much.

We decided to take Dane out alone that night, instead of joining the team for dinner. Dane, with his usual forthright way of talking, asked us if we wanted to know what he'd been doing since he'd left home four days earlier. He proceeded to give us a day by day accounting of practices, meals and funny anecdotes. It was just what we needed to pull us out of our funk. This is what was happening now. Look at how much fun this was! Dane was playing in a Junior Olympics tournament!

I had given each of the boys a letter before they left and included the poem "Don't Cry at my Grave." We were able to reach both Brady and Graham at camp on their cell phones. We told all the boys how much we loved them and how we all carried Ryan in our hearts.

Bruce and I left Tucson on Wednesday. It felt like we were leaving Ryan there. Since Dane's team was still playing and they had a "bye" that day, we decided to take an earlier flight home and drive up to camp to see Graham and Brady. We both were anxious to see them. We stopped at the cemetery and were absolutely overwhelmed by the loving remembrances left there by his friends and family.

It was a short drive up to Club Wilderness, just a little more than an hour. We were hoping to see a campfire while we were there but we really just needed to connect with Brady and Graham. It was so good to see them both. As we were leaving, Graham gave us this letter:

Dear Mom and Dad,

Why? That is a question each and every one of us asks of ourselves everyday. The answer is because it was time for Ryan to become an Angel. I truly believe that everything in life happens for a reason; so while we are all stuck down here, Ryan has moved on to bigger and better things. He always had to be first to do everything.

The last thing Ryan ever said to me was, "Graham, you know I'm gonna die today, right? I don't know how to ride a motorcycle, this is the last time you're ever going to see this beautiful face." HE WAS LYING, GUYS. I believe in my heart that there is a wonderful place beyond explanation where Ryan and Grandpa are waiting for us, and one day we will all be reunited together.

Dad, Ryan and I would often talk about how close the two of you were. When you two argued, I think it was more of the fact that Ryan wanted to be in charge as opposed to him to him really being mad at you. He truly cherished all of the time he got to spend with you in Colorado, at the River etc. Know that he watches over us everyday and he loves you very much.

*Mom, many of Ryan's friends would often come up to us and remind us that we had the coolest mom in the world. Ryan would sort of shrug his head in agreement, con-*scious, of course, that he had to keep up his cool image when responding. We would often talk about how lucky we were to have parents like you guys. You made a comment at Counseling one night that just because you and Ryan fought, that didn't mean that you didn't love him. Well, that doesn't mean that he didn't love you either, Mom. Ryan loved you very much and still loves you. He was just too *prideful to admit it sometimes.*

We all need to remain strong and know that Ryan is still with us. I love you and miss you guys.

Graham

Bruce and I both recognized, in this letter, Graham taking over the role as the oldest child. He reached out to both of us, trying to be comforting. He referenced my concern that the boys would misunderstand my love for Ryan because he was the child who challenged me the most. I used to always say, "Twenty-five percent of my children, seventy-five percent of my parenting." The truth is, I was very hard on Ryan in lots of ways. He was hard on me too! He was my first child. I was less experienced and more idealistic with him than I am with any of the other boys. Ryan truly forged the path for his brothers. I had become concerned, after Ryan's death, that the boys might misunderstand the intensity of our relationship and question the love we shared.

Bruce and I were incredibly touched by Graham's letter. I will keep it forever. He was now the oldest brother and he was bringing to this new role, incredible insight and compassion.

We had made it a year and we were all okay. We were Ryan's survivors.

He Was My Best Friend

*The fondness by which one is remembered is the
greatest mark a person can leave upon this Earth*
Author Unknown

Ryan could have written the book on friendship. He
understood that being a friend was the very best way
to have friends. So many people claimed Ryan as their
best friend, that Ryan's ability to connect with people is
immortalized.

E-mail sent to Ryan by Josh Needle on June 26, 2000,
the day after he died Read by Bruce at Ryan's service:

Hey guy,

*I love you buddy. You had such an impact on my life.
When I was growing up, I wanted to be you, you had it all.
I had no confidence in myself, but you made me believe in
myself. You pushed me along, raised me up and made me
want to be me. Many times I tried to tell you how much you
meant to me and how you helped me become the person I
am, but you would just say, "Naw, you did it yourself." I'll
never forget the time when you told me you were proud of*

me, how you thought I had things all figured out, when most of my life, that's how I felt about you. I could have never repaid you for all that you have given to my life. I just knew that we were supposed to grow to be old codgers together, still telling stories and reliving the days of our boyhood, growing up...the river, camp and all the stupid things we did. Well, I'm still gonna grow old with you. I'll just relive all the memories I have with you, and smile and know that you're smiling down at me.

I never have known anyone who had such a positive impact on so many lives. I think about the impact you had on my life and how you made a difference to so many others in so many ways. You had a winning personality and a million-dollar smile that could warm anyone's heart and make them feel good.

I learned a lot about life from you. There are many things that we did together that are gonna hurt me to do in the future cause I'm gonna miss you so much. I will carry on and be strong because I know you'd be ticked at me if I slowed down for a second. I know you're always gonna be there standing next to me, mumbling out of the side of your mouth pushing me to exceed my potential.

I love you so much. I will miss you and remember you for the rest of my life.

Ryan was everyone's best friend. He understood what it took to truly be a friend and that is his legacy. With his passing, we all understand how precious life can be.

Uncle Taylor's poem for Carter,
read by Candi at Ryan's service

Happy Birthday Ryan, My Friend

My friend has gone far away from this land I miss
the precious touch of his loving hands.

Give your friends a hug, maybe a kiss
Because one day, they will be missed

His smile is gone but it was very kind
His laugh is silent, but not in my mind

To everyone he brought a touch of sun.
We were buds and had lots of fun

I never knew yesterday was our last day. I
thought I could look at my friend, hug him and
say: "I love you, Happy Birthday!"

Don't let one day go by without telling him
How you love him! Remember you may not
have another year to be with him.

All I have now is great memories, A heart full of
love and eyes full of tears To remember our fun
throughout the years.

Now I have to look up at the stars and say,
"I miss you, Happy Birthday!"

All I have now is great memories of our time at the
river He was my friend and my soul mate,
and now he's gone down river

He will be with the current, always going
down river.

Tomorrow will come and be gone without his voice.
I will remember our fun, because it is my choice.

I will always wish that in June I could be with him.
In spirit and mind, I will always be with him.

Now when I think of that June day "I will think
to myself, Happy Birthday"

Please remember when you pray, to thank your
Heavenly Father up above. For the friend He
gave you with so much love.

My friend, my cousin, my soul mate is gone down river
His smile, his laughter, and his spirit are up river.

To remember Ryan, all you need is a smile With
a laugh and a sparkle in his eye His spirit will
always be alive.

Epilogue

When Ryan was only three years old, my mom made him a red Superman cape with a big felt yellow "S" on the back of it. He loved it and wore it everyday. I can still see him flying around our house and backyard with his halo of curls and knobby knees.

Years later, Ryan, by then in college, asked me if I could find his Superman cape. He was going to a costume party and thought the cape would be perfect. He could dress his still-knobby knees in tights.

You can't imagine Ryan's disappointment when I produced the cape.

"What happened to it? It was always so big."

"It was big, Ryan, but now you're bigger."

I am the mother of Ryan at every age and these are the precious memories. I just never thought my memories would end at twenty-one.

So much has happened since the first anniversary of Ryan's death. The summer of 2001 was the "Summer of the Heatstroke." Corey Stringer's untimely death sparked new interest in this phenomenon. He died from the same complications which cost Ryan his life. Corey's death was the most publicized because he was famous but there were many, many deaths from heatstroke this summer. It gave us an opportunity to; once again, explain what happened to Ryan and to educate people on heatstroke.

Graham left for Arizona State University in August. It was hard to see him go but, as Dane told me, "It's the right thing for him to do. It's the right time in his life." He loves it. April is getting married.

Then September 11th happened. Our whole nation was mourning and continues to mourn. President Bush led the nation by asking us to continue living. It is what we have done on a very personal level. It is the right thing to do.

Another family who had lost a child wrote to us after Ryan's passing. In the letter, they included this passage from Judith Viorst's book Necessary Losses.

"Perhaps the only choice we have is to choose what to do with our dead: To die when they die. To live crippled. Or to forge, out of pain and memory, new adaptations. Through mourning we acknowledge that pain, feel that pain, live past it. Through mourning we let the dead go and take them in. Through mourning we come to accept the difficult changes that loss must bring—and then we begin to come to the end of mourning."

In the very beginning, I found it so odd that the living family members were listed as "the survivors" because it seemed so very obvious to me, that learning to survive would take quite some time. It is an unfinished journey but we have traveled far. We are more accepting now, less raw, less tortured. Bruce and I feel that we have turned a corner. That which was agonizing a year ago, is no longer so painful. We are in a very different place. We have taken Judith Viorst's advice to heart. We choose to live our lives zestfully. We choose to have Ryan be our guiding angel and live our lives as joyfully as he did. We choose to be survivors.

In Loving Memory of Ryan Bruce Ferguson

"Ry-Guy", "Fergie", "Stick", "Hahn", "RB", "Fry-Guy", "Rhino"

Our Very Best Christmas Present December 25, 1978 to June 25, 2000

Cherished Son of *Pam and Bruce* **Devoted Brother of** *Graham, Brady and Dane* **Loving Grandson of** *Jeanne, Carol, Art, Hal and Arlene* **Adored Nephew of** *Candi, Taylor, Nan, Bob, Jim and Susan* **Treasured Cousin of** *Travis, Crosby, Carter, Sarah, Christopher, Parker, Conner and Mackenna*

Some people believe that God gives us the gift of some special people for a very short period of time...

Ryan, and inspiration to all who were touched by him, friend to all who knew him

Memorial Service

In honor of Ryan Bruce Ferguson

June 29, 2000 at 3:00 P.M. Trinity United
Presbyterian Church 13922 Prospect Avenue,
Santa Ana, CA 92705

Order of Worship

Welcome and Prayer
Pastor Bob Pietsch

Scripture Reading
Pastor Jeff Wagner

Romans 8:31-39 John 14: 1-6 Song: *Wind Beneath
My Wings* sung by Wendy Stephens Eulogy God's
Words of Hope

Pastor Bob Pietsch Song: *Softly As I Leave You*
sung by Wendy Stephens Closing Words
Pastor Jeff Wagner

Irish Blessing led by Wendy Stephens The Lord's Prayer led by Wendy Stevens Benediction *Pastor Bob Pietsch*

Pallbearers:	Honorary Pallbearers:
Graham Ferguson	Travis Grant
Brady Ferguson	Crosby Grant
Dane Ferguson	D.J. Mumford
Carter Grant	Matt Boone
Brady Journigan	Mike Vogeding
Marc Hickman	Josh Needle

A burial service will immediately follow at Holy Sepulcher Cemetery.

In lieu of flowers, please make a donation to the Ryan Ferguson Foundation
P.O. Box 3212 Orange, CA 92857-0212

The family expresses their gratitude to the worship leaders:

Officiating: Bob Pietsch and Jeff Wagner Musicians: Wendy Stephens, Dave Gundlauch & Fran Johnston

A special thank you to the many relatives and friends who have expressed their love and support to the family.

"Ryanisms"

He could never talk fast enough to say everything
he wanted to say…why say "mom" when you could
say "mom, mom, mom, mom, mom"

"Definitely", "For sure", "Yea buddy",
"Yeahhh", "Let's get it on"

After screw-ups..."Wasn't that great?" "No one
is more disappointed in me than me," "You
check your credit card bill?"

Ryan...

Born Christmas Day, 1978 at Hoag Hospital in Newport Beach, California, the first of four sons of Pam and Bruce. Shortly after Ryan came along, the young family moved to Villa Park, where Ryan lived his entire life in a wonderful family-valued community.

Growing up was filled with adventure, family, and friends. From pre-school to college. T-Ball to varsity baseball, Bluff Lake rookie camper to veteran counselor, Ryan lived life his way. He loved family vacations, Indian Guides, Snow Skiing, Snowboarding, Water Skiing, Music (especially Dave Matthews), and of course his Truck—he loved it all, every minute of every day.

At the family place at the Colorado River, Ryan started in diapers, coping with rocks, bugs and dirt. He learned to water-ski at 3 and jet ski at 7, and by 10 he could drive the boat. At 16 he could fix just about anything and everything that broke, and something always did. By 18 he was mature enough and responsible enough to start a whole new generation of tradition at the river, bringing his own friends on his own.

From his infamous knobby kneed perspective, Ryan saw the world through eyes that saw things on the bright side, and a smile that said it all. It was that smile that first drew people to Ryan. They stayed to enjoy his sense of humor, and share his zest for life, earning Ryan a richness in friends beyond his years.

Through Orange YMCA Camp Bluff Lake's "Ragger" Program, Ryan tied his most personal goals to his "brown rag," symbolizing his commitment to bettering himself. One of the shared goals amongst all "raggers" is to "...look up and laugh and love and lift." Always holding this sentiment close, Ryan kept a tattered copy of Footprints in his wallet.

One night a man had a dream. He dreamed he was walking along the beach with the Lord. Across the sky flashed scenes from his life. For each scene, he noticed two sets of footprints in the sand; one belonging to him, and the other to the Lord.

When the last scene of his life flashed before him, he looked back at the footprints in the sand. He noticed that many times along the path of his life there was only one set of footprints. He also noticed that it happened at the very lowest and saddest times of his life.

This really bothered him and he questioned the Lord about it. "Lord, you said that once I decided to follow you, you'd walk with me all the way. But I have noticed that during the most troublesome times of my life, there is only one set of footprints. I don't understand why when I needed you most you would leave me."

The Lord replied, "My precious child, I love you and I would never leave you. During your times of trial and suffering, when you see only one set of footprints, it was then that I carried you."

Secrets of Motherhood

The very first kick I felt was strong and powerful
I should have known then, what a presence you
would be But I still thought I was the mom, older
and wiser with love to give And that all the teaching
would be from me.

I was so ready to be a mom, so educated, so well-
read The first thing you taught me was how little I
knew As I tried to shape your character and teach
you values I couldn't even figure out how to show a
leftie to tie his shoe!

By the time you were seven, there were four little
guys So I watched carefully and do you know what
I learned from you? Boy stuff, and all about soccer,
snowboards and pitching toes, Why a balk is called
and the infield fly rule.

But did you know that I have also been a pitcher?
Every time you took the mound, every strike-out,
each breath-taking feat

My heart was with you, helping you hold the ball
Learning about true character and competition from
my son, the athlete.

Now graduating from high school, you are moving
ahead with your life I see the poise and the
confidence you possess And I thank you for all the
secrets of motherhood you taught me Remember
I love you as you keep reaching for each new
success!

Congratulations! Love, Mom
June 12, 1997, High School Graduation

Irish Blessing

May the road rise to meet you May the wind be always at your back May the sun shine warm upon your face And rains fall softly on your fields. And until we meet again, May God hold you in the hollow of His hand.

The Lord's Prayer

Our Father who art in heaven Hallowed be Thy name. Thy kingdom come, Thy will be done On earth as it is in heaven. Give us this day, our daily bread And forgive us our debts As we forgive our debtors And lead us not into temptation But deliver us from evil For Thine is the kingdom And the power and the glory Forever, Amen.

2010...Not the final chapter

It has been ten years since Ryan died and our family has grown in our acceptance and adaptation to this loss; and the boys have grown up! Graham graduated from Arizona State University and married Christi Contois; a beautiful, kind, philanthropic, thoughtful young woman. Brady graduated from San Diego State University and spent one college summer study at Oxford University. Dane pitched on CAL's baseball team and graduated from Berkeley in 2008. All the boys are working in career jobs.

Travis and Sharie now have two darling kids, Tanner and Hailey, and still live in Boston. Jim and April have two little guys, Grant Ryan and Benjamin, who bring such joy to our lives. We have lost a brother-in-law, Bob Mitchell; Bruce's mom, Jeanne Ferguson and my dad, Hal Brasure. Losing Ryan has given us a permanent perspective on the difference between a loss and a tragedy. Too many families in our close circle have lost young people tragically. We especially remember Scotty and Shari Meyer, Nick Sammons, Cyrus Allizadeh and Brandon Clairmont. We hold these families in our hearts and prayers.

Bruce's diabetes is well managed by exercise. He has added ocean kayaking in a surfski to his hobbies and tries to go out two to three times weekly all year. My Graves Disease affected my eyes when I was writing this book and my vision became vertically double. My surgeon said that losing Ryan probably made the Graves take a ballistic course since it is an autoimmune disease and stress impacts the autoimmune system dramatically. I had three neurological surgeries over fourteen months and my vision improved from being double ninety-five percent of the time to being single ninety-five percent! Thank you Dr. Peter Quiros. Please stay under a doctor's care. Medical problems may be mistaken for grief and grief exacerbates physical symptoms or underlying conditions.

We sent this letter to our family and friends
on Ryan's tenth anniversary

The Ryan Ferguson Foundation

Ten years ago, we established the Ryan Ferguson Foundation. We wanted to honor Ryan's memory by supporting two of his passions, Camp and baseball. We thought this would be Ryan's legacy. We didn't understand then how much we would receive with every donation.

To date, the Ryan Ferguson Foundation has given away more than $45,000 and we have enough money in reserve to continue gifting at this rate for many more years. Both the Orange Y.M.C.A. Campership Program and Villa Park High School Baseball have received the majority of the monies through annual contributions. As the Foundation grew, we were able to donate to additional causes that we, as a family, agreed to support. The Foundation contributed to CAL Baseball, World Vision and Casa de Amma, a residential treatment home for Special Needs young adults. We have supported research for the cure of Cystic Fibrosis, Juvenile Blindness and other debilitating childhood diseases. After Hurricane Katrina, we contributed to the American Red

*Cross and the Foundation donated to the families of firemen who were killed on duty. In one especially proud moment, we helped to pay for some of the burial costs of a young dad who had died suddenly. The Foundation also supports the gifting of <u>Surviving Ryan</u> books to families in need, as well as Ryan's website, **www.ryanfergusonfoundation.com**.*

The Ryan Ferguson Foundation is supported by the generous donations of family and friends, all the sales and royalty checks from <u>Surviving Ryan</u> and proceeds from Creations for a Cause note cards. We thank all of you.

We believe that we honor Ryan's memory with each contribution the Foundation makes and that he is smiling with that famous crooked grin. Ryan's true legacy seems to be to teach us all how to "Pay it forward".

Much Love,
The Ferguson Family

*****

Time has really helped our healing. Ryan is always remembered and is a part of our family celebrations. On May 16, 2009, Graham and Christi were married. Brady and Dane were co-best men and Ryan was listed in the program as *the missing best man.* Before the wedding rehearsal, Christi called us all together in Graham's room for a meeting. We thought this was for all the parents but it was just our family. *"I can't imagine what this is like for all of you to do this without Ryan and I wanted you to have something special today."* She gave Bruce and the boys silver cufflinks with a picture of Ryan alone and the four brothers together. Christi gave me a broken-heart necklace with Ryan's birthstone. This is one of the many reasons we love her and we thank Christi for again making us a family of six here on earth.

Since losing Ryan, my practice has expanded to specializing in grief, especially parents who have lost children. My personal experience gives me a very different perspective and I have learned so much. There is no good way to lose a child but some ways are much more difficult. When a child dies at the hands of another, the grief and anger are almost one. If a child dies accidentally because of a parent's actions, the guilt tends to overwhelm the grieving. Suicide tends to leave the parents, family and friends tormented by what else could have made a difference in saving the child. My initial research at the time of Ryan's death said that losing a child through illness is the easiest of this most difficult of losses because the grieving starts earlier and isn't such a shock. My work doesn't support this premise. Parents, who lose a child to illness, saw their child suffer and experience pain and so the preparation for death is always at odds with the hope there will be a cure. There is no good way to lose a child, but the parents who seem to have the hardest time are the ones without faith because for them, their child's death is the end of their time together. God's Law of Predestination helped me to make peace with losing Ryan. It was just his time and I know we will all be together again.

Remembering Ryan always helps us. A close friend who recently marked the first anniversary of his son's death was perplexed and hurt that people didn't remember. For a parent who has lost a child, this is a very personal September 11th, a day never to be forgotten. **There is no reminding the grieving.** Mention their child and if they cry, they cry because their child died, not because you remembered. We still celebrate June 25th as a day to remember what happened to Ryan because the rest of the year we try to honor Ryan's memory joyfully. It is a sad anniversary for us and we were very surprised at how hard the tenth one was for each member of our family. There has been so much change.

Elizabeth Kubler Ross' five stages of grieving were originally meant to describe the journey of how one faces his own death. I believe that resilience is the most important factor in surviving one's child and I choose to be resilient. As Brady recently said, *"…sometimes we choose everyday and we take comfort in little things."* The only choice we have is how we are going to handle difficult times. God doesn't promise us a life without challenges but He does promise to be with us everyday. In my final letter to Ryan, I asked him to lend me one of his smiles until I could again find my own. I have found my smile. I choose to live everyday fully and cherish my relationships until I am with Ryan again.

Ryan, you have shown us all,
In your absence,
How precious life can be

Breinigsville, PA USA
09 February 2011
255237BV00001B/2/P